To the ladies who made this possible.

Thank you Hanna Lee and Alison Woodward.

PROLOGUE

THE MARS FELICITY STATION had a bleeding wound—a hole in reality that burned with green fire and leaked horrors into the world.

Wicked, white-and-gray, eyeless things crawled through, dripping with an oily black ink that Mark Rufus had theorized to be *the blood of the universe* minutes before he died.

Oh my God. They're terrible.

Those were amongst the last thoughts that rolled through Mark Rufus's head. Now they were a part of a stream of consciousness that echoed inside the great beast.

The Harbinger.

Many had come through the gate, each unique in its horror, but all submissive to the greater beast and he had many titles.

First born. Voice of the mother. Herald of her will.

Harbinger of her hunger.

Each of the other beasts had a mind, and each connected to his.

The Harbinger's purpose was not like that of the lessers—those that lived for meat and blood—no, his was not a mission of hunger and destruction.

But of submission.

Folding into himself, limbs cracking and snapping into small frames to lessen his great size, he stepped through the burning, bleeding gate and into the new world. The blood that flowed through the veins between worlds leaked upon him and ran down his thick hide and chitinous shell. The blood of the universe felt warm, as it always did.

With him, the voice of the queen traveled. She spoke to him, and her desires became known, just as he had made his known to the lessers.

The lessers bowed their heads in submission as he entered into the world. They quailed to the floor for fear of the Harbinger and his great strength.

Cords of muscles bounded and rippled up his terrible form as he exited the gate and uncoiled himself within the new world.

His was a mind that reached and touched, feeling the world. It was a sensation unknown to many other beings.

He had been first of his brood to crack through the thick, rigid shells of the cluster. He'd come into the world screaming and vicious. Before her mind had reached him, he was a chaotic thing, falling upon his brothers as they emerged behind him, weak and tired from the struggle of birth. He sunk his claws into them, killing without mercy and feasting on one for as long as it took another to emerge. He did not rest. He did not sleep. He only killed until none remained. The scars of that struggle were upon him still. The struggle had lasted ages.

And then she spoke to him.

Words calmed the chaos within him and brought purpose to the terror of his existence. When his mother spoke to him, she took from him but gave so much more.

He was no longer one, but many. A single shell may house him, but he felt and touched through many minds.

And he did. The blood from the hole—in reality, the world wound —dripped off him as his mind reached.

This world before him was strange, as the unconquered worlds always were. It was cold, and the atmosphere was thin.

Before long, a blubbering creature native to the world was brought before him. A long, red smear trailing in his wake.

Man.

The Harbinger understood it, even if the term was alien to him. The memories and minds of the *men* already brought to submission flowed through him, though they were still vague and difficult to comprehend.

This was *man*. A small, soft creature that cried when afraid.

It had been dragged before him and dropped—a gift, an act of submission by the lessers.

One of the Harbinger's arms extended from the folds of his body and plucked up the flailing *man*.

The *man* screamed, but those sounds of suffering meant nothing to the Harbinger, as he was born to a world of suffering and the words were not yet something he could comprehend.

Bone, cartilage, and muscle tissue shifted and moved, cracking and popping, upon the Harbinger's head as his structure reformed. His new eyelids popped open with a wet snap, and his glassy black eyes inspected the *man*.

The *man* screamed again and again, an unending howl of fear.

The Harbinger watched the *man's* chest rise and fall as it gulped in the atmosphere. Slowly, he began to understand.

Paralyzed with fear, the *man's* cries shriveled into silence as the Harbinger's body—evolving and ever-changing—began to shift and crack once more.

The flesh upon the Harbinger's face tore open as deep holes formed into nostrils. They flared as the Harbinger took his first breaths.

The *man* began screaming anew.

1

"Line up!"

Commander James Tealson had heard it from somewhere deep within, a memory echoing from when he was a younger man. At twenty-something, he'd felt old, but he knew now how foolish he'd been.

It was strange the things you remember when you think you might die.

"Tealson, you fall in line, goddammit!" the drill sergeant had bellowed.

That was a voice that pulled him even further back in memory.

He'd spent three years after high school working odd jobs to save money for college, intent on avoiding the life his father had led.

Intent on not being a grunt for life.

Two years into college, the little money he'd saved dried up nearly as fast as the bills grew. The pretty girls and the appealing drinks had just been too much. Drowning in debt, he'd dropped out and signed his life away to the U.S. government. It was unfair to say the debt was the only reason. It was just the kicker. Too much drinking and too little studying was the disease.

The U.S. Army was the cure.

"You get a nice sign-on bonus," the recruiter told him. "*Few years in, we'll help you with that college debt.*"

So, yeah, he felt a little old standing next to the smooth-faced recruits who came in right out of high school.

"*It'll make a man out of you,*" his father had told him, pride filling his voice as he balanced his weight on a cane. He'd needed the cane ever since his tour of duty in Venezuela. Some fourteen-year-old had hurled a frag grenade that put shrapnel in his leg. "*About time you grew up.*"

And grow up he did.

"*Yes, sergeant!*" was burned deeply into his skull. He'd even been told he occasionally mumbled it in his sleep.

It was only a few months into boot camp when he heard Orbital Corps was taking hands out of all the other branches, so long as they volunteered.

"Shit, why the hell would I want to be in Orbital Corps?" his friend, Jason, said. "All those idiots do is sit up in space and scratch their balls."

Sit? Scratch balls? That was music to Tealson's ear as he crouched on his knees, scrubbing the floor with a toothbrush.

Turned out he was a natural. As natural as you can be at hauling cargo around and not pissing off too many people. It was back and forth to the space stations and the moon base with an occasional trip to a farther base, like Mars.

There had been some real excitement when they were talking about mining asteroids, but Tealson wasn't interested. A little more than a decade in and he was already captain of his ship. Plus, he had gotten to know the people in his crew pretty well, so why the hell would he want to change things up?

He had some leave back on Earth, and he just happened to see Jason out at the grocery store, himself on leave. They met up and shared a beer together, reminiscing about their days in boot camp. He heard stories about invasions and bullets, about insurgents and ambushes. The wars weren't just across the globe anymore.

Sometimes they were popping up in the good ole' U.S. of A.

"Fucking Comanche..." Jason said before trailing off.

Tealson listened the entire time, but all he'd thought was, *Should have followed me on up, Jason.*

Something had happened between here and there, the man he was and the man he'd become. Something Tealson himself hadn't *quite* realized at the time. He'd changed. He was another person entirely. He just shared the same name as that dumb asshole who signed up for Orbital Corps because he thought it'd be easier.

But he was only certain of it when he heard about his father passing.

Nothing.

That's what he felt. Nothing really at all. A dull and numb sense of *nothing.*

He'd talked with his father a few times a year, maybe as little as two times. Of course, Tealson forgot a few birthdays, but he always made sure to call on the anniversary of his mother's death.

He didn't hate his father. He loved him, sure, but he was someone else than he'd been before.

It was just the same skin.

The rationalization was cold, along with the decision not to attend the funeral.

He sent flowers to his sister. He wasn't sure if that was a thing people did or not, but figured he should. It was probably the least he could do, while still being able to sleep soundly at night.

They hadn't talked since.

James Tealson, captain of the *Perihelion*, still had a family though. It just wasn't the one he was born into.

"Hey, Commander," Joseph DalBon said in their last poker game. *"I'll raise you this nudie mag and this pack of peanuts against your thermal socks."*

They laughed their asses off when Linda Stalls took the hand. Ever the card shark.

"Welcome back," he said another time as he extended his hand to Yui Tanaka, fresh from maternity leave. "You miss us?"

"I'm glad to be back." She cracked a grin, ever composed, and came aboard the ship. He'd hated the Japanese before he met her. He'd been raised on his father's memories of the invasion of Tokyo and the occasional pieces of advice like, *Watch those Japs. They'll kill you for the nickels in your pockets.* It wasn't until Tanaka he'd understood how everyone was the same under all the external bullshit. They all had families, and they all had lives they wanted to live.

Tealson's family was stuck inside the same tin can as him, hurtling through space.

Ben Halsworth, or "Bennie" to everyone on board, for one. Despite knowing how to irritate the shit out of him, there were few others Tealson liked to share a beer with. And of course Stalls and Colton Parker. The two had been with him ever since he became a captain.

They were family.

Mike Burns might have been family to him, too, if he'd stayed long enough. If Tealson hadn't had to beat what was left of Burns to death.

It was a damn shame. He'd been a good kid, if annoying at times. He'd talked back on occasion, but had known where the line was.

Tealson was walking on a line right now—right down the center of it inside his ship. But the line wasn't rules and regulations, it was the line a man walked for fear that if he stepped off, he might not be a man at all anymore.

He might just crack and fall apart.

Duty. That's why Tealson loved Orbital Corps, even if he hated it at the same time. He was good at what he did. Always was. Even back in boot camp, he hated it, but he made sure every officer there knew he was dedicated.

Duty was why they were here. He hoped his crew would understand that. They had a duty, not just to Orbital Corps and its mission, but to every man, woman, and child who called themselves an American.

That was why he couldn't turn tail and run.

Duty.

There was a high-value asset in Mars' Felicity Station. It didn't matter that he was almost certainly dead. Duty demanded they know for certain.

Will Braun. Genius scientist and high-priority asset. Is he worth it?
No. He wasn't.
That didn't matter.
He had orders and intended to carry them out.
Now, standing here, walking the line between his crew members geared up on either side, he hoped they would understand.
Duty.
"You've all already heard what's down there, but here's the rundown of what we know," Tealson said. He didn't make eye contact with any one person. "Unknown entities are infesting Felicity. Parasites that have taken over former crew and staff. They are now considered hostile. And Reeves. . ." Tealson glanced at him and then away again. "He reported that something bit Burns. It was when he got infected. Close contact can initiate infection."

"*Fuck*," someone moaned.

"Here's what's going to happen," Tealson said, ignoring the complaints. "Parker is going to prep the CAGs in cargo, and you're all going to get equipped. You're authorized for lethal engagement."

"Sir?" Jeff Regal asked. "Who is gearing up to board?"

Tealson stopped to look him down. "Just get your shit on."

Cameron Elliot snorted out a laugh. "You kidding? Me? I'm a goddamn *environmental specialist*. I don't know a damn thing about rifles or combat."

"I work cargo, Elliot," Parker said. "Ain't one of us that's equipped for combat."

"What about Tanaka?" Elliot pointed at her. She was staring down, her back stiff and her face emotionless. "You sending *her* out too?"

"Everyone's getting a job, and I expect you to do yours." Tealson huffed, getting closer to Elliot. "You make me repeat myself again, and I'll make you the pointman."

The crew's booster engineer stepped forward. "Sir." Barry Smith's voice was far more flat and weak than he'd ever sounded. "You know he's dead, right? We don't need to go down there. Will Braun is dead."

"Smith's got a point," Elliot said, snapping his fingers. "And if he's not dead, *fuck'em*. He is a *Nazi*."

"Doesn't matter if we think he's dead or not. Our orders are to go in and make the attempt. Besides, there are others living down there. Will Braun is priority, but we're the only chance for every other person stuck in that hell. You'll get your CAGs. You'll be fine."

No, they won't.

Tealson froze halfway down the line. What was that? A nagging, doubtful voice in the back of his skull?

Oh, no, that's just a cold sense of reality telling you that you're marching in undermanned with crew undertrained.

Tealson frowned. His crew didn't need a captain who was doubtful; he could see it on their faces. They needed one who *believed*.

But he didn't.

Duty.

He found the word and focused on it. If he could hold it, he'd squeeze it until it cut his flesh and blood dripped down his fist.

Duty.

He looked them all over, fighting back an uneasy quelling deep inside his gut.

They can do it. Let them know they can do it.

"Before command ever had you set foot on a ship, what did you do?" Tealson barked. They looked around, confused and unsure. "*What did you do?*" He repeated, louder this time. He searched them for one who would remember.

"Rifles?" Tommy Reeves asked.

Tealson nodded. "Before you ever set foot on a ship. Before you ever learned how to wire a comms system or check environmental data, the Corps put a rifle in your hands. Each trooper is a rifleman before he's an engineer. Before he's a mechanic. Before she's a medic. *A rifleman.*"

They're not ready.

There was that voice again. That *fucking* voice.

He ignored it.

Make them believe.

"Why in the hell did you join Orbital corps?" he said as he paced up and down the line. No one dared answer him. "Was it because you wanted to do something new and exciting? Well, what's more exciting than being the first person to shoot an alien in the face?"

2

CLOSE WAS NOT a great word to describe Alice Winters and her father. He loved her, she was sure of that, but he didn't always show it—and that was putting it kindly.

That craving for *just* a little more attention led her to beg to join one of his hunting trips when she was just eleven years old.

"You see it?" he'd asked her in a hushed whisper, pointing into the brush.

The deer had gone still, a part of it knowing it was being hunted just by the stillness of the woods, the gravity of death reaching up to hold it *just* in place.

She lined up her rifle, looking down her scope as her father had shown her, all the while silently pleading with the deer—*just move, just run.*

There wasn't any part of her that wanted to kill it.

She only wanted her father to be happy.

But it didn't move. If anything, it grew more still.

"Take the shot," her father prompted.

In haste, she didn't squeeze the trigger but jerked it. A part of her had fully desired to mess up the shot.

The blast echoed through the woods, and the deer started jumping and—

No, it hadn't.

She couldn't imagine, even still, that it had jumped and ran away. That her father had smiled and told her everyone messes up their first shot, and that they were going to have to work on it more. They'd have gone home empty-handed, laughing at how badly she'd missed the shot, and then they'd spend more time at the target range.

Because she hadn't missed.

She watched with trepidation as the animal kicked, bucking in the air before taking a few wobbly, uncertain steps, and finally collapsing to the ground.

Cold fingers of guilt slid into her chest and squeezed her heart.

"Good shot," her father had said as he patted her back.

What happened in the moments that followed, she wasn't sure. She didn't remember standing up and walking to the deer or what else her father said. If it had been a dream, then she had shot it, heard her father's praise, and then was standing over it.

But it wasn't a dream—it was a memory. And she could only remember staring down at its dying eyes and broken jaw where it had smacked into a tree on the way down.

"Damn," her father hissed. "It wasn't a clean shot." Were his words sympathetic? Were they sad? They seemed that way...

The deer's chest rose and fell, and its jaw opened and closed. Its tongue hung out.

Die. Please, God, just die.

She remembered that part clearly. Praying God would snuff it right there.

He hadn't.

"You have to shoot it, Alice." Her father had pointed down at its chest. "Right there."

Shoot it. Kill it. End it.

It wasn't fun. It wasn't a game. It was painful, and it hurt.

She hurt.

Her arms trembled from the weight of the rifle as she raised it. She lined it up, but her fingers were weak. "I can't," she'd said to him, choking back a sob.

She wanted him to do it. Her father could line it up and shoot. He could kill it, which somehow would be better because she wouldn't have to do it. She hadn't meant to do it at all. It had only been for fun.

It wasn't fun.

The woods were silent. Every bird and every insect had been struck dumb and quiet from the rifle round, and they all waited patiently for the scene to unfold.

"Alice," her father had said as he put a hand on her shoulder. "You know what my favorite thing is about you?"

He spoke, but she barely heard him. It was like a distant conversation, one from the next table over at a restaurant. The words were there, but they were quiet against the wheezing breath of the deer.

"You've always done what was right. You never take the easy way out." His hand had squeezed her shoulder. "You're not weak."

And then, impossibly, he'd turned and walked away. She'd heard the crunch of leaves as he left her there.

With the deer.

The thump of her heart was just like the tick of a clock. Each beat announcing another second of agony the deer was forced to suffer.

Her hands had been cold, and her fingers had been numb.

But she'd lined up the shot and pulled the trigger.

Her father was right.

She wasn't weak.

Now, for some unknown reason upon the Perihelion, she was thinking about that time—the deer's eyes vivid and clear in her memory—as she suited up with her Combat Armor Gear. It had taken both Tommy and Moller to help her properly fit, first pulling on the skin suit that went beneath it and then locking the metal armor pieces in place. Each piece buzzed to life as it connected to the circuit of the weapon's system.

Jet black, sleek, and inches taller, she felt strong and heavy. She knew the power of the CAGs, how she could now kick through a door or drag a full-grown man up a hill with ease.

She'd worn one while on tour in Tripoli, and looking around the group, she imagined she was the only one who ever wore a CAG during combat when the bullets were flying and people were screaming.

She knew how it felt when a bullet ricocheted off the CAG. She'd taken one directly in the head. It had hit with such force that she'd had a bruise and headache that lasted a week, but she'd lived.

Everyone was trained, so everyone knew what it felt like to wear one.

But being trained and being tested... they weren't the same.

Her CAG had a metal badge indicating she was a medic. That badge doubled as an emergency scan key to be used when or if the security systems all became operational again. She knew Felicity Station's staff could open doors via retinal scans, but for her and the *Perihelion* crew, badges would suffice.

They geared up and moved into the docking bay with Tealson. It was the largest room on their ship, which made moving around in the bulky suits easier.

It had been a long time since she'd seen so many men and women in armor. A long time since she'd felt the gears of war begin to turn.

Bennie and Stalls, the flight team, stood in the corner. Stalls's arms were crossed and Bennie's hands planted firmly in his pockets. Alice thought they looked out of place when surrounded by the armored troopers.

Alice carried her helmet at her side, her hair pinned tightly to her scalp. She exchanged a look with Tommy as he snapped his helmet into place. It sat on his head for half a second before the automation came on and pulled it down, air compressors popping as it locked into place.

His eyes were cold, as cold as her own. There was something said between them with that look, but neither voiced it out loud.

She placed her own helmet on her head and heard the gears whine as internal magnets connected and pulled it down, locking it into place.

They kept looking at each other, and Tommy leaned in, pressing his visor to hers. When he pulled back, he tipped his head down and she did the same.

You can do it. We can do it.

Her father had been right. She was scared, yes, but anyone in their right mind would be.

But she wasn't weak.

"Elliot, grab the other side of this," Tealson said, still suited in his polished black CAG. He held up a paper grid map that was covered in dust. "Help me roll it out." Elliot walked across the room and grabbed the end of the map, rolling it out for Tommy to look over.

Well, Tealson has changed, Alice thought. He'd aged a decade in just a few hours. She hadn't known him long, but he'd always been a kind man, easy and even. The type of captain who helped unclog toilets.

The look in his eyes had shifted.

That wasn't him anymore.

"All this for a Nazi?" Tyler Bartlet asked. "This is bullshit."

"Bartlet, shut your damn mouth," Tealson warned. He pointed to the map and looked at Tommy. "Listen, Reeves, these maps are old and are likely from at least two renovations ago, but you've been down there. You know more or less what this place looks like. Based on the wiring, where do you think they'd most likely keep the cryo beds?"

Tommy was nearly indistinguishable from anyone else underneath his helmet. The badge indicating "electrical engineer" was the only distinguishing feature. Alice watched as he marched over to Tealson and leaned forward onto the table to look over the map. He aimed a finger down at a dense cluster of electrical cables. "Cryo beds eat a hell of a lot of power. They're also not easy to just pick up and move around. Based on this wiring cluster, they could be here, here, or here." He pointed at three different locations.

"Give me your best assessment, trooper. Which location?" Tealson asked.

Tommy looked at the map for a few solid moments before he tapped his gloved finger onto a spot. "If I was the engineer during the renovations, I'd have them right here."

Tealson leaned in to look more closely and nodded his head, so Tommy continued, "You can see how the wiring is all going back from that room," he traced a finger along a line on the map, "to this grid here. I'd bet there are at least a couple dozen beds wired up in that room."

Tealson's gaze traced a route on the map. "Mostly a straight shot, if we cut through the cafeteria."

There was an itch on Alice's back. One of the irritations of the CAGs. She couldn't even scratch it. She blinked hard and tried to ignore it. She'd seen men go half insane from the *crawl*. It wasn't a term used in any textbook, but every medic who'd had boots on the ground had seen it.

The CAGs had cooling and heating systems, created to maintain a comfortable atmosphere. In practice, though, it was far from comfortable. Cool as it could be, sometimes stress made people sweat. A drop might roll down the side of a trooper's face and then another. Adrenaline would make their heart beat like a high-powered piston, and then sweat would roll down their back. At this point, their skin would begin to *crawl* underneath the armor.

If it went on long enough, Soldiers, Troopers and Marines would even complain of feeling like insects were inside, *crawling* across their skin.

She'd seen a man in Libya panic, saying something had gotten inside his suit. Half mad, he'd pulled his helmet off, even as Alice yelled at him to put it back on.

Rounds peppered them as if the insurgents had been waiting, knowing he would remove his helmet and expose their target. A round cracked his head open, and he'd laid on the ground screaming as Alice—

Stop it.

She tightened her fists. Her mind was wandering again. She'd come out here, into the cold vastness of space, to try and get away from those thoughts and memories, but wearing the CAG made it all come back.

Focus on the task at hand.

She keyed in on Tommy, who was still talking, "—entirely possible the base is leaking fluid and oxygen. We'll need a full reboot with the generators." He pointed to the map. "Otherwise. . ." Tommy shook his head. "We're at risk of this entire place decompressing from a stray shot."

"What do you mean?" Tealson asked.

Elliot laughed cruelly. "He means the entire place could *pop*. We're going into a fucking powder keg. Decompression means everything starts blowing up. Oxygen tanks, cryo tanks, nitrogen—"

"*I get it*," Tealson snapped and pointed a finger at Elliot. "Stow that shit." He looked back at Tommy. "If you reboot, we'll get airflow and reset the power through the facility? It'll bring up the security functions and reduce the chance of decompression?"

Tommy shook his head. "In theory. This whole damn place was designed in the eighties and hasn't been updated for some time now. Resetting the power won't make us decompress, but I can't make predictions for what else might happen."

"*Shit*," Tealson hissed and shook his head. "And we need to go back into the goddamn power room where those fuckers got Pax?"

"No, we can reboot directly at the generator. We have to head down into the maintenance shaft and do a hard system reboot."

Tealson considered carefully, and let out a sigh. "All right, we're breaking into three teams. Bennie, Stalls, Moller, and Tanaka are staying on the ship. Now, half of you have already been in there with me, and you know they don't die easy. We're going to need every gun we've got, so I don't want to hear any damn complaining."

"I can go too," Tanaka said, holding a CAG helmet but not yet suited. "I'm just an information systems technician. I'm no good on the ship, and I'm trained just as well as everyone else."

Tealson looked her over, silent for a moment before he nodded. "All right, go get suited up." While she walked away, he looked to the others. "Bennie and Stalls are keeping the ship warm. Moller," he said, tipping his head at her. "You're going to do everything you can to see if you can clear the signal interference. Everyone else, we're breaking into two groups. Half are going for Braun, and half going for the reset."

Tommy nodded in agreement.

"Sir?" Alice said, stiffening up. Tealson nodded to her. She came close to the map and pointed at it. "Look at the schematics." Alice tapped her finger on the generator corridors. "It's meant for maintenance staff. We're going to be shoulder to shoulder down there. What happens if some of them *do* get down there, and we all start tripping over each other? We'd be better to have fewer people here, and—"

"What happens is we stomp a mudhole in their ass," Elliot interjected. "We're wearing CAGs, Winters. It's not that hard to underst—"

"Do you *ever* shut up?" Tommy sneered, straightening up.

"Both of you, settle down." Tealson raised his lips, showing teeth. "Elliot, you step out of line again, and I'm going to break your fucking neck." Tealson gave him a hard stare that finally forced Elliot to look away. "Winters, what were you saying?"

"This is a tight, two-man, shoulder-to-shoulder corridor made even smaller with the CAGs." She tapped a finger down. "It'll be a kill zone if we get stuck in here. Numbers would actually be against us. Too many down here will just mean more confusion. We should split the groups seven and four."

"She's right," Tommy agreed. "Besides, the team moving through the base will need more firepower."

Tealson nodded in agreement. "All right. Winters, you're leading the team."

Alice was aghast. "Me, sir?"

"That's correct. I read your file. You did a few combat tours, and you've got a good head on your shoulders. You're in charge of the reboot group."

"Sir, I'm just a medic."

"You're a medic, he's an engineer, and he's a sensor calibrator." Tealson tapped his knuckles on the table. "Get your shit together, Winters. You're taking the lead." He looked across the people there. "Smith, Reeves, and Bartlet, you're heading with Winters." Tealson continued, "The rest of you are with me. Go get your rifles."

Alice looked over at the others. Peter Becks stared blankly at the ground. Colton Parker idly rubbed the outside of his helmet. Then her gaze settled on Moller.

The girl looked like she was about to have a heart attack.

Every hand holds a rifle.

She'd heard the phrase before, but she didn't know where it came from. She knew the meaning though.

When the time comes and the need is there, every hand holds a rifle.

The group broke apart and everyone secured their positions as the flight crew took on manual control for the landing.

It wasn't long then before they'd re-entered Felicity.

The ship rocked gently, and even though they all knew it, Stalls announced: "Ladies and gentlemen, our surprise return trip to Mars Felicity is a success."

3

WILL BRAUN WAS THINKING. The gears inside his chest turned and clicked, a quiet ticking only he could hear.

He was otherwise silent in his contemplation.

The others were panicking, spitting meaningless words and exerting unnecessary energy as they paced about the room.

Braun was thinking.

Numbers, odds, and possible outcomes played out in his head. He tested each the way a carpenter tests his creation—holding them and judging for balance and weakness.

An uneven plan would topple and smash.

And many would die.

Braun stared at the wall. People walked in front of him, but he heard nothing. He was down in the labyrinth of his own mind, lost deep within its corridors.

In his mind's eye, the map of the space station stretched out. He saw each tunnel, each hallway. He predicted where vents were and where they would stretch to.

And what things may come out of them.

Layout. We are on the other side of the compound. The gate is near the center of the facility. The rescue team is in the docking bay.

Hostile factors?

Mechanically, his hands steepled in front of him and rested just in front of his lips. He often did this, unintentionally, when thinking.

Creatures. They will have fanned out. Due to recent disturbances in the power room, they will have focused, possibly toward the bay location. Rescuers, not expecting the circumstances, will be loud and incompetent.

Many of them will die.

Idly, he scratched the edge of his chin, which was no longer flesh but a synthetic skin weave he'd had installed some years ago.

They will draw the creatures' attention, thus reducing threat levels in this region. However, it would be unwise to assume a total reduction in threat levels.

Best course of action?

Take advantage of rescuers' distraction and reduction in threat levels.

Execution plans?

Braun's breathing stopped as nearly all faculties of his mind focused.

Direct movement toward rescuers?

Negative. Threat levels uncertain in center region of facility and precarious in bay region. Hostile entities will cluster there. Direct movement will result in traveling through uncertain regions and directly into abundantly hostile regions.

Indirect movement toward rescuers?

Considering. Threat levels reduced in outer regions as focus drives toward rescuers.

However, the threat level remains high in bay region.

Other considering factor? Gate is functioning. Creatures are still entering our reality through the bleed.

Indirect movement non-useful if creatures continue to fan from center. Rescuers' actions may not distract hostile entities. May instead proceed to random locations.

Group members also suspect. Likelihood of members to make noise and break from fear at inopportune times? High. Likelihood of refusal to carry out plans when threatened? High.

Trustworthy? Negative.

Indirect movement still viable with hostile factors and untrustworthy companions?

Negative.

He began breathing again. A man came by and tried talking to him, but Braun was deaf to his words and didn't bother to acknowledge him.

All series of movements calculated and deemed impassable.

Wait in secure location for possible rescue attempt?

Positive factors? Group members' preferred action. No need to travel through uncertain regions of the facility.

Negative factors? Rescue team will not arrive. All advantages from their distraction squandered. Facility failure and decompression. Room not as highly secured as anticipated.

Feasible to wait for rescue?

Negative.

"Hmm." This was the only sound Braun had made for quite some time. It likely relieved the room to know he was not dead.

Movement toward rescuers, unfeasible. Awaiting rescuers, unfeasible.

Next potential course of action?

Braun slowly looked up and scanned across the room. "Are any of you electrical engineers or knowledgeable about the facility's wiring?"

No one answered. They just mumbled amongst themselves, and a few couldn't peel themselves away from looking out the window.

"I, uhh, I understand the electrical wiring for basic mechanical maintenance." It was a woman with black hair, which curled at the ends. She was breathing deeply with each word, clearly terrified. "I'm an engineer in—"

"What is your name?"

"Dixie Messing." She looked particularly young to be an engineer. She likely accepted such an undesirable position to help advance her career.

Best course of action? Take advantage of rescuers' diversion to penetrate gate region. Recruit Dixie Messing in helping to disable or temporarily diminish gate capacity and prevent further increase in creature presence.

Gather a greater understanding of creatures and common practices to best navigate facility and prepare next course of action.

Hostile levels? High. Urgency in disabling gate? Necessity.

Logical to proceed amidst uncertain factors?

Positive.

Braun stood up. He clasped his hands behind his back, watching each member of the room before settling. "I've got a job for you, Dixie."

"Quiet," Braun whispered and held up a hand. A creature—one that had come through the gate and not one that had taken human flesh—had moved just ahead of them. They'd rounded a corner and saw it slinking away.

Braun had noticed, with particular interest, that it had no eyes and no discernable ears. Beyond that, it had no evident genitalia.

Fascinating.

Some things could be deduced. The lack of sex indicated likely reproduction through eggs, but it was the lack of sensory organs that was the most puzzling.

They likely had an unknown sense.

Possibly they sense through vibrations and acute feeling within their skin.

It was a thought to consider, but not at the moment. Now he had to focus.

After the creature had moved away, Braun spoke, "Okay. Go." He pointed to a corridor, and Dixie raced across to it. He followed behind her slowly, treading through water that was, annoyingly, shin-deep. They passed by large, exterior windows showcasing the landscape of Mars. The sun was rising in the distance and painting their shadows against the wall. Braun was thankful for that, as the power was still only semi-functional on this side of the facility. The blinking emergency lights offered little help for actually seeing.

They had left the group back in the room. Braun knew the layout of the station well enough, but he still didn't feel particularly confident moving about in the halls with those abominations running around. They reached a 'T' intersection at the end of the hallway, and Dixie turned around and held up her hands as if to say, *which way?* Braun pointed to the right, and Dixie nodded. He admired her willingness to be useful.

It was rare to find those who could be useful.

The lab was close, but Braun was getting uncomfortable. He shivered, the cold water making his skin prickle. He'd done what he could to ignore it, but without proper clothing, it was making the muscles in his legs tighten. Breathing was hard too with the air not properly recycling. It tasted as if the filter had gone bad months ago, and Braun could imagine it was leaving a thin coating of filth on his throat.

He coughed to clear his throat.

Down the hallway, something crashed. The sound of breaking glass? Braun wasn't sure. It had come from an open room, presumably some staff member's room.

Braun and Dixie froze in place.

Slowly, as if it were playing through a movie, Braun watched as a hand, red with dried blood, reached out and grabbed the frame of the door, pulling the rest of the body through the water. He'd seen only the reaching tentacles before he grabbed Dixie and pulled her into a room alongside him, another living quarters. The door was cracked open, and blood was on the wall.

Someone had died here.

Dixie huddled close to Braun, and he still had his hand tight on her arm.

"*It was one of them,*" he whispered to her. "*One of the men.*"

"It's coming this way," she said through clenched teeth. "I can hear it."

Braun could too. He imagined its tentacle dragging across the glass window. He could hear the long, squeaking sound it made.

"It's going to come in here, Braun," she said to him, pleading for a plan.

"No, it's not," he hissed back. "Just be quiet."

But it kept coming, the long, dragging noise. They saw the water swish as it got closer.

It was going to come in.

Braun pulled her back carefully in the room. There was a kitchen counter that they could hide behind and wait for it to pass.

They hunched down behind the counter, the water rising up above their waists. Dixie squeezed in, a fearful desire to make them both as small as possible.

It was in the room now. Braun heard its fingernails tap on the door frame. Was it playing with them? It inhaled and groaned painfully as it exhaled .

Wait for it. It'll leave. Just wait.

It didn't leave. It drew in closer, and now the sun shining through the doorway cast the creature's twisted shadow near them.

Dixie leaned in, her teeth practically inside Braun's ear. "*It's going to find us.*"

Braun nodded in agreement and reached into a nearby cupboard and came back with a soup can. "When it passes," he said. "Move. Quickly."

Braun tossed the can into a bedroom, and it clattered against a desk inside.

The creature shrieked and rushed through the water.

They saw only its back. A black, ripped-up T-shirt and a single tentacle stretched out from behind and curled forward like some terrible, man-sized earthworm.

Go.

Just as it passed, they burst up and slogged around the counter and through the door. Braun glanced back only enough to see the creature's mangled face, its cheek and chin ripped open and raw, as it came behind them.

"There!" Braun pointed ahead to the laboratory, the thick metal door was hanging open. He heard the creature bang around behind them but didn't look back.

Dixie got ahead of him, rushing inside and got behind the door just as Braun got through.

Immediately, she slammed the door. Braun turned and pressed his weight against it, but his feet were unsteady against the slick, wet floor. The creature slammed against the door and knocked Braun back, splashing water as he fell on his ass. "Help me!" Dixie screamed, managing to stay on her feet.

The tentacle had gotten through, and the man's fingers were clawing in. Braun jolted up and got to a cart, grunting as he shoved it in front of the door. Dixie moved away as Braun held the cart pressed to the door. The emergency lights in the room flashed continually, making the room go from dark to light every half second.

"Just hold it!" she yelled.

Braun groaned from the weight as the tentacle slipped inside between the crack of the door. It closed in by his face, stretching as far as it could and rubbing against his chin and leaving a slimy residue as it looked for a place to pull or choke.

It slithered up to his lip, and Braun could see the creature's face amidst the blinking emergency lights. It pushed one eye against the crack in the door to see inside. The eyelid had shriveled up, and it looked to Braun as if the eye might just roll out at any moment.

"*Hurry,*" Braun choked out, straining with all he could to hold the cart in place.

The tentacle slithered down his face, but he dared not pull a hand away to swat it away. It hooked around his lip, trying to peel it back and enter into his mouth. If he leaned back at all, the door would burst open.

Something cracked and snapped behind Braun, splintering like broken wood, but he couldn't look back to see.

Screaming as she rushed in, Dixie shoved a piece of broken wood between the crack of the door, catching the creature in the face and knocking it back. Its fingers stayed tight and curled on the frame.

Dixie smashed the wood back and forth, but it wasn't stopping. It didn't seem to mind having its face speared.

"Let go. It's not working," Braun said between clenched teeth. "Just help me."

Dixie got alongside him, and they both groaned, shoving the cart as hard as they could. The tentacle began to shake and spasm in the air as it was squeezed by the metal door. Pushing harder still, blood leaked from the tentacle as it was pinched.

Breaking through the skin, the door finally shoved harder, cutting through the tentacle. It flopped around uselessly, still stuck by strands to the creature outside, as the door slammed into the creature's knuckles.

The small bones crunched and popped as the door snapped them off, and they fell into the water. The tentacle squeezed like a tight sausage in the door, pulping out and shaking like a dead fish as the door locks snapped into place.

Gasping, Dixie said, "What the hell are those things?" She stood with her hands on her knees, clearly struggling to stop herself from shaking.

"I don't know," Braun said, and that was true. But he had theories.

He sloshed through the room, taking in all he could with each flash of irritating light. "We're trapped in here." It was not said from fear, but only as an observation. A problem that needed to be solved.

"Look here," Dixie said. She'd booted up a vid-screen. "The whole system is dead. Lights are off, but the computer systems are functional. Most of the connected systems are down. This whole shitty place is standing on rotten legs. It needs a reset."

"Let me see," Braun said, taking the controls.

He clicked through several screens, and the word *NONFUNCTIONAL* appeared over and over again. He brought up the security cameras, and they seemed to be working in some portions of the facility.

"Hmm." He typed in commands and hit enter, bringing the camera to the power room.

The entire room was flooded, but the lights were still on there. There were creatures there, and these weren't like men at all. They were demons that had crawled out of nightmares. Beings from an alternate reality. Braun knew he wouldn't be able to shut off the power to the gate room. Not this way. The gate was going to stay on.

"*Scheisse.*" Braun's lip curled in irritation. "We can't get close to it."

"No," Dixie said. "But the cables run through these walls." She looked up to the ceiling. "If I can get behind those panels, I might be able to damage one of the conduits enough that it will short out. With the power malfunctioning like it is now, it should be enough to disable it."

We heard a knock.

Why was he thinking that right now? How could it possibly be helpful?

Because the beings are smart. You heard them before. They knocked, and you answered.

"Braun?" Dixie asked. "You still with me?"

It wouldn't stop them. It would only slow them. He was sure of that.

"Okay," he said, regardless. They'd made their move, and now he would make his.

She climbed onto a counter and began pushing on the tiles above. One dislodged, and she slid it aside. She looked down at him. "Just don't leave while I'm up there."

"Indeed, I will not, mein fraulein," he said, and she grabbed onto the ledge, pulling herself up and crawling inside. "Careful, that you do not stray from the metal structure below your feet. The ceiling tiles will not support your weight."

She looked down at him. "There's room up here for maintenance and wiring. I've been up here before."

Braun waited, hearing her scuffling and moving above.

The tentacle caught in the door began to lazily lift and jerk, then the creature thumped its fist on the other side. Apparently it had regained its wits.

At least this one doesn't moan.

He considered that as it kept a rhythmic thumping against the door.

"I got it!" Dixied yelled from above. Then, moments later, "*Braun,*" her voice was meek now, afraid. "I think something is *up here with me.*"

It sent a chill down his spine.

"Come back down the same way you came," he called. He heard a shuffling from above, the sound of Dixie sliding over the tiles. But there was another noise, scuttling, like tiny suction cups being pushed and pulled in rapid succession, skirting across the tiles quickly.

No.

He looked around the room quickly, for something, anything, he could use as a weapon.

Just help her get out.

Braun jumped up onto the same counter Dixie had used to climb up. He looked at the hole and knew he didn't have the strength to pull his entire body up as she had.

It didn't matter.

First, there was a scream, but that quickly turned into a choked sound, the air suddenly leaving her lungs in a quick punch, as she no longer had the *ability* to scream. Then Braun watched as blood ran in rivulets down from cracks between the ceiling tiles and splattered across the front of his pants as it splashed off the floor. He leaned back, truly frozen in place as something thumped against the weak ceiling tiles.

He had been right. They couldn't support her weight.

The tiles cracked, and Dixie's disemboweled body crashed through, unraveling from the ceiling to the floor in a bloody strand of intestines. Dixie's face was locked in a perpetual scream, and for a moment, Braun reached out to her as if he were able to somehow save her, but only for a brief, illogical moment.

Given the choice, he would have saved the girl. He took no pleasure in death, but neither did the cold metal engine in his chest feel much discomfort from it.

It ripped her in half in only seconds.

Braun noted that cruel piece of information as he leapt off the counter, splashing the water. He decided to move before he too might get ripped in half.

But, if he were honest with himself, Dixie still looked alive. Her eyes had that glimmer of a heart still beating and lungs still drawing breath.

It was as if her body had yet to realize it was dead.

He reacted coldly and swiftly as her dying eyes watched him. He got to the side of the door and opened it. The insane creature missing its fingers bolted inside immediately and closed in on the closest meat.

Dixie.

She was still useful.

Braun stepped around it and headed out the door. He looked back and saw the creature notice him just as he closed and locked it inside the room.

Braun hoped the girl's life had bought them time. That she had been able to disable the gate.

If she had, then it was a life well spent.

He turned and sloshed through the flooded hallway, against the rising sun filtering through the windows to Mars to once more rejoin his group.

4

Tealson huffed inside the bulky armor, as he still wasn't used to walking around in the CAG. It was calibrated to be easily adjustable, but Tealson always felt an extra spring in his steps. Knowing he could leap a standing six-foot vertical with ease, also made it hard to get used to. It was easy to miscalculate the strength and push a little too hard, and be thrown entirely off.

The whole thing felt like a horror movie as they stepped into the base. The front entrance was well-lit but flooded up to his shins. But when they separated from Alice's group and veered off in the direction of the cafeteria, they were back in the dark and the blinking emergency lights.

With each flash, the lights seemed to whisper, "*Danger, danger, danger.*"

"Goddamn things are more irritating than helpful," Peter Becks remarked, huffing and shaking his head.

"Mmhmm," Colton Parker agreed. "You'd almost rather it was full dark and we could just use the headlamps."

"*Fuuuck* that idea." Elliot snorted out a laugh. He had his rifle locked into his armpit and was ready to raise it. "I'll take half lights over no lights at all."

Tealson was taking point, as he didn't feel right asking anyone else to do it. The water flowed around his legs, but to where, Tealson hadn't a clue.

Hopefully, everything starts to kick on in this fucking tomb.

He looked back and noticed the expressions on the faces of his crew. Everyone seemed tense, unsure, and nervous.

They should be.

"Listen up," he said, addressing his team, knowing morale was the duty of the commander. "You're all trained for combat."

But not for this.

"There's nothing here you can't handle. Nothing this *armor* doesn't equip you for. You stay tight, listen to orders, and you'll be back on the ship in no time."

There were grunts and nods, but no one spoke.

"We're not worried about what Winters and her team are doing. Our mission is to extract Will Braun and any other living soul." He turned around, facing deeper into the facility. "Follow me."

They headed in, making good progress until they hit a large corridor door. Tealson moved to where the locks could scan his badge, but it was as he feared.

Locked.

Tealson pointed to a panel. "This side of the grid is still down. We're going to have to pop everything open."

"Hey, wait a minute," Parker said as he moved to a wall. "Let's get one of these shutters up, let some light in." Parker dug his fingers underneath a metal shutter against the wall.

"The hell are you doing?" Elliot asked. "You pull that up, and you'll break the whole damn thing."

"Guess they can bill me." Parker grinned back at Tealson who nodded. He let his rifle sag on his shoulder as he groaned, cranking the shutter up.

The sun had risen over the horizon. Light from outside spilled in, and they all saw the barren, orange landscape.

"I'm going to feel a hell of a lot better when we can get those up and these damn lights off," Peter Becks said.

Tealson appreciated the light and gave Parker a nod. He then looked to DalBon. "You're up. Get over here and pull the switch."

"Sure, make the fat guy do the grunt work," DalBon joked as he handed Parker his rifle. He stripped off the panel and grabbed the underlying handle. Putting one hand on the wall for extra leverage, he yanked up, but the handle barely budged. "Goddamn thing is *frozen*."

"Must be pretty solid if you can't get it with the armor," Tealson said as he leaned closer to the door-window to look through. It was dark inside, but he could see the cafeteria in between the flashing lights.

"Let me make a go at it," Becks said as he sloshed through the water. He laughed a dry chuckle as he slung his rifle over his shoulder and jokingly spit into his hands, rubbing them together. He planted a foot next to the wall and grabbed the handle with both hands. He groaned, and the added strength from the armor caused his foot to crush part of the wall. Grinding his teeth, Peter kept pulling until the handle snapped completely off and he tripped and fell backward, landing on his ass. "Damn thing is frozen!"

"That's what I said, dipshit." DalBon went over to offer Becks a hand up.

"Heating must be dead on that side," Tanaka said. "Cut off in that room altogether. Froze the internals there."

"She's probably right," Elliot agreed. "We better wait until the reboot and let it warm things up some."

"Like hell." Tealson pointed at Becks. "Light your torch and burn us a way through."

"*Confirmed*," Becks said sarcastically, but he was grinning as he got the small handheld torch out of his pack.

"You should know better, commander." DalBon patted Becks on the shoulder. "Don't you remember when this dumb asshole about set his bed on fire trying to light a fart last year? Never let him play with fire."

Ignoring him, Tealson issued orders. "Tanaka and Parker, you two keep eyes on our six. I don't want anything sneaking up on us. DalBon and Regal, help Becks cut the door. Elliot, just shut the fuck up for a bit."

"Roger that," Tanaka said, holding her rifle awkwardly.

Before long, Becks had cut enough of the door that they could kick a hole big enough to shimmy through.

The chunk of metal landed on the floor on the other side and threw up a splash of water.

Tealson was the first one through, the barrel of his rifle held up as its light shined through the darkness. The water rippled from his movements. There were rows of tables inside the large room. Tealson shined his light across them.

Becks came in and moved to one of the cafeteria's tables, inspecting it. He held up a tray of food. It looked old and dry. "Food was probably still warm when whatever the hell happened to them kicked off." He set the tray back down.

They were surprised.

"Yeah," Tealson agreed. "Something happened, and when it did, it happened fast."

"Sir?" Tanaka said, and Tealson looked back at her. She scanned her rifle light across a wall. "There's blood."

Specks of blood. Splashes of it. Tealson definitely wasn't a blood-pattern specialist, but he knew a spray pattern when he saw it.

"Oh, there's shitloads of *blood*." Elliot nodded sarcastically as if he was intrigued. "But no *goddamn* bodies. What the hell happened to them?"

DalBon also flashed his light up and down the walls. "Elliot's got a point. It's weird to say, but I think I'd be a *little* more comfortable if there were some corpses."

"There won't be any corpses," Tealson said flatly. "Didn't you see what we're dealing with? They get back up. They *all* get back up."

"*Hey*," Becks said. He let the word hang in the air for a moment, as if he was afraid to even ask. "How many people were in this facility?"

"One hundred and fifty," Tanaka answered. "Give or take. Could be more if they had their families here. The records aren't clear."

The water started to slosh around on the other side of the room, and a loud screeching began.

"What in the hell..." DalBon said.

Tealson felt his heart clench and the muscles in his arms tighten.

He hissed, *"Rifles up."*

5

Being in charge held a weight that Alice firmly felt on her shoulders. Nothing—in her opinion—qualified her to take the lead.

You're the only one who's seen a bullet wound. The only one who's been in combat.

Focus.

They'd had to go to an access hatch and crank it open. It'd taken Tommy and Bartlet together to get the damn thing to turn. Without the assistance of the CAGs, they wouldn't have had a chance. With it popped, they'd taken a ladder down into the internals of the Felicity base. And while the above-ground portion of the base had white walls and a sterile but comforting look, the lower levels did not. Everything was cold and black, and portions had begun to rust inside the waist-deep water.

"Everything just keeps getting worse, doesn't it?" Tommy said. Alice knew the water shouldn't have leaked down here. It was sealed off from the rest of the base to keep critical structures intact in case of a worst-case scenario.

Apparently, the engineering hadn't held up.

"You get some asshole back on Earth with a pencil and a piece of paper designing the shit up here." Smith snorted. "Dickheads always think they know what they're doing. What a bunch of morons."

"Oh yeah?" Bartlet remarked. "They're the stupid ones? Look where you are, dipshit. They're still on Earth, and we're the ones doing this bullshit."

Alice couldn't disagree.

Water was leaking down from the ceiling. The loud dripping reminded Alice of the rainstorms from back home. The water swirled and waved in the corridor, continually flowing into the darkness.

It was pitch black, and only their rifle lights and headlamps guided them.

"This is some bullshit," Bartlet growled as he pointed his light ahead of them. "Fuck this goddamn Nazi."

"We don't have to like him—we just have to follow orders," Tommy said.

Bartlet looked back at him and scoffed. "You want to take point, then?"

"I'll walk point," Alice said, shoving past Bartlet. "You just watch our asses. Tommy and Smith, you stay in the middle."

"Works for me," Smith said, watching her pass.

"Shouldn't be too far down here," Tommy said, flashing his light down the corridor. "We'll come to a maintenance box and can reset it there."

"You don't think the water's fucked it all up?" Smith asked, doing his best to trudge forward.

"Shouldn't have, but who the hell knows anymore?" Tommy remarked.

"You know the goddamn Russians did this, don't you?" Smith said as he shined his light across the ceiling. "Wouldn't surprise me in the slightest. Germ warfare. Popped something in the air ducts and let it go crazy."

"Sounds like a movie. A stupid one," Bartlet said, his voice flat. Alice snorted out a laugh. Bartlet continued, "You know what, though, I hope that water did fry this whole thing. I hope this whole place is fucked and fit for scrap so we can just write them all off for dead and get the hell out of here."

"*Shit,* man, that's unAmerican," Smith said, looking back at him. "I hope we just flip this switch, get Braun, and then let Earth send a squad of Marines up here to clear this place out. After that? I say we pay the Russkies a little—" Smith trailed off and stopped.

Alice looked back at him. "What is it?"

"Goddamn, it's cold down here," Smith said.

"You're imagining it." Tommy elbowed him and prompted him to keep going. "You can't feel a damn thing through the CAG."

"Yeah. . ." Smith looked over to Alice, but she could see the worry in his eyes. "Yeah, I guess."

"You good?" Tommy looked him over, and Smith nodded.

They kept on until they got to the maintenance box. They formed around Tommy as he went to work. The corridor stretched farther, and Alice flashed her light into the darkness.

"*Hey.*" Smith smacked his hand down on her shoulder, and she looked at him. "I can feel something in my suit. Something is moving."

He's got the crawl.

"It happens," Alice said. "Your body is itching. Tucked tight in there you can feel something moving around. You have to try and work through it—ignore it."

Smith nodded.

Over his shoulder, Alice noticed something bobbing in the water about fifteen yards away. She froze.

What the hell is that?

"*Shit.*" Alice hissed. "Over here! Rifles up!"

Tommy came alongside her, pointing his rifle in the same direction.

"Not you, Tommy," she barked out. "Get the reset."

"There's something inside my suit!" Smith said, standing alongside her with his rifle pointed. "I can *feel* it."

"There's not a damn thing in your suit!" Bartlet snarled. "They can't get through CAG like that!" He flashed his rifle light down their direction. "Fuck this, I'm not letting that thing get close."

"Wait!" Alice commanded. "We don't even know what we're firing at yet."

"*Goddammit*," Bartlet cursed, but held firm.

Whatever was in the water shifted suddenly. It was too much for Bartlet. He fired a round, and the flash of rifle fire lit up the corridor.

Alice's eyes went wide, but she held steady. "Did you hit anything? I can't see shit!"

"I don't know," Bartlet replied.

Tommy snapped the box closed behind them. "I'm done. It might take a while, but it should kick on. Let's get the hell out of here."

"Get down!" Bartlet shouted, causing Alice to duck into the water as a spray of bullets fired over her head.

She hadn't seen the one above her.

"Be careful!" Tommy yelled. But there was another shout, a terrible, fearful noise.

Smith.

A long tentacle had wrapped around his throat and yanked him into the air. The CAG armor was strong enough that it didn't choke back his screams.

"There's another one!" someone said, and there was more firing.

A creature had come up from the water. It had a thick, bulbous head, but no eyes. Thin arms with white flesh lined with red veins, and long fingers reached for Alice, but a stream of rifle fire cracked into its face, sending it back into the water.

"I hit it!" Bartlet shouted. "But the fucker is underneath the water now!"

Alice could almost feel it. It would swim close and grab her legs. It would drag her under and pull her helmet off. She'd scream, bubbles bursting from the water, and then its big mouth would latch onto her face and tear through her head with one bite.

It might do that, but it hadn't yet.

She was still alive, and Smith was in the air.

"Train your fire on that one!" She hadn't waited for the others. She only raised her rifle and fired. The rifle fire illuminated the creature crawling on the ceiling. It had eight or more legs, each thin and pointed with fingers at the tips, clinging to the wall. A large mouth opened wide as its reaching tentacles felt down for Smith, trying to drag him in. The others joined Alice, and the bullets slammed into Smith and bounced off him as they hit the creature. The impact made Smith jolt and squeeze his rifle, and he accidentally sent a burst of fire down on them.

A bullet slammed into Alice's visor, cracking the glass. Another hit like that, and it'd break through and take her eyes.

The creature on the ceiling pulled Smith between itself and the fire and moved away. Its tentacles slid and oozed between his CAG pieces as he fought. It pried them up with the sounds of twisting metal and fit its mouth toward his arm.

Smith screamed as Alice watched the creature's jaws work in a sucking motion.

"Kill it!" Alice roared and continued to fire.

"Reload!" Tommy called out as he stopped and ejected the clip, slapping another one in.

"Come on, you ugly shit!" Bartlet yelled as he let out another burst that did more to hit Smith.

"Careful, dammit, or you'll kill Smith!" Alice yelled at him. "Hit *it*, not him!"

The creature from the water burst out and clung to the wall. "Hih-ht," it barked. "Hihht it! Hihht it!" The thing jumped off the wall and collided with Bartlet. He worked a hand up and wedged his thumb into its mouth. It bit down, and Bartlet screamed. She imagined the thumb tearing off.

But it shouldn't have gotten so close.

Alice pushed the barrel to its head and pulled the trigger.

Round after round hit its skull. Alice saw each of them as they impacted. The creatures were strong, and the first bullet popped the flesh and made its head jolt. The second tore through the muscle. The third cracked into the bone.

It turned and hissed at her, and Bartlet shoved his rifle into its mouth. When he pulled the trigger, its entire head rocked back, and it fell. Bartlet's hand came out of its mouth, the CAG armor having saved his thumb.

Alice snapped her head up and saw Tommy still aiming at the one on the ceiling. It still had its mouth clamped down on Smith's arm, making him scream.

"Blow its fucking tentacles off!" Alice called.

They all trained their rifles again and fired.

That had been enough.

The blasts hit the tentacles holding Smith, enough that they burst and hurled out black blood. The thing went weak, and Smith fell to the ground, slamming into the water, a flopping tentacle still wrapped loosely around him.

"Keep it up!" Tommy yelled as they kept firing.

Whatever went through the creature's mind—whatever its thought process was—it had decided that it had enough and went fleeing down the corridor, still effortlessly clinging to the ceiling.

Smith burst up from the water. "You got it! It let go!" He laughed in defiance. "Mother. . . fuckers!" Tommy helped pull the slimy tentacle off of Smith's suit.

"Bitch!" Bartlet screamed after it. "You pussy!"

"Let's get the hell out of here!" Tommy slapped a hand on Bartlet's shoulder.

Alice looked away from them and to Smith. "Come on, let's go. We need to—" she stopped mid-sentence, her breath catching in her throat.

Smith was holding his arm, and he looked from the wound to her, his eyes wide and scared.

The creature had gotten through. It had bitten his flesh. She saw the blood.

It could already be inside him.

The parasite is latching onto its host.

Just then something shrieked, and Alice snapped her head in that direction. More voices joined the shrieking.

They were coming.

"Fall back!" Alice yelled as they retreated.

6

XTU RIFLES WERE standard issue among combat units in the early days of Orbital Corps. Although less favored by other branches of the U.S. military, the rifles were chosen by Orbital Corps for their superior ability to fire in extreme weather and atmospheric conditions.

Such considerations weighed heavily on the minds of those who foresaw a space war that never happened.

Ultra-lightweight materials and superior design led to a stunning weight of approximately three kilograms even when fully loaded with its thirty-seven round magazine and five round oversized buckshot under-barrel addition.

"You know what this is for?" Tealson's training officer had asked as he tapped the under-barrel addition of the XTU, which for all purposes made it a passable shotgun. "This is for when the motherfuckers get up close."

Tealson was thankful for the oversized buckshot and the under-barrel addition he now gripped tightly.

Because the creatures were getting *very* close.

They had come screaming from around the corner, beneath the flashing emergency lights that hadn't been lying when they silently whispered, *"Danger, danger, danger."* It was a suicidal swarm of once-men that moved like a flood of arms, legs, claws, and teeth. A mob with a single purpose.

Kill.

They tore through the knee-deep water, sending small splashing waves at the Orbital Corps Troopers. The first of the swarm came with arms outreaching, and the ones behind clawed for the front.

They howled and screamed, painful and tormented sounds of agony and despair. It was as if they had felt the fires of Hell and wished to share the secret.

The cafeteria lit up with rifle fire, and strobing light revealed the gnashing teeth and blood-coated fingers.

"Cut them down!" Tealson roared, pumping the action on the XTU and blasting oversized buckshot into the front line.

Red mist. That's what the creatures became as the oversized load sent hundreds of ball bearings, each approximately a third of an inch, screaming in their direction.

The blasts ripped arms apart and took heads from shoulders. Reaching tentacles disintegrated into sludge that splattered on those behind them.

But death and pain were of little concern to the swarm. Not with their secrets of Hell and burning. Not with their hunger for flesh, and their desires to feed.

A naked man rushed Tealson's crew, his bulbous stomach split open and something with insectile legs reaching from it.

Rifle fire ripped him in half.

A woman, purple and black as if bruised and beaten, had her hands clenched up to her chest, her head swinging loosely and a tentacle sprouting from her mouth. A ripple of bullets climbed her leg, breasts, and face, throwing her back into the crowd.

"*They're not dying!*" someone screamed behind Tealson.

He knew that. He saw it with his own eyes.

One with a mouth twice as wide as it should be and filled with snapping pointed teeth rushed the line and got too close before Tealson could pump the action on the XTU and load one of his few remaining buckshot rounds. Instead, Tealson held his arms up, pivoted his ankle in the way of a man who knew how to throw a punch, and hurled his fist forward.

It went between the creature's reaching arms and connected with its chin. The impact shattered its teeth and turned its whole head around.

Tealson even heard the *crack-crack-crack* as the spine snapped apart. The loss had disconnected some necessary wiring inside the body, and it went limp, ragdolling to the floor. It came up seconds later, and Tealson imagined the parasite's horrible wisps crawling through the whole body like puppet strings.

He kicked it hard and, with the power of the CAG, sent it skittering across the floor.

Snapping his rifle up and sneering with hatred, Tealson held the line as the rifle rocked and sputtered in his hand.

"*Shoot them in the head!*" another person yelled. "*It's not working!*" someone else said almost instantly.

The once-men came, climbing over the broken but still living bodies of the fallen before them. They cared nothing of pain or destruction. Heads blew off and still, they kept coming.

They don't even know what fear is.

Colton Parker roared as he grabbed an arm and ripped it off, using it to bash another of the things in the face.

DalBon stomped his heel down on one that had fallen, caving its chest in completely while it reached up to grab around his knee.

Tanaka was silent as she had the rifle locked into her armpit, leaning forward and picking her shots as the flash of rifle fire lit up her pitch-black armor.

Tealson grabbed a table with one arm. It was bolted to the ground, heavy and thick, and meant to seat at least twenty people. Grunting, and with the strength of the CAG, he tipped it up and threw it in front of them. The swarm crashed against it, climbing over even as their arms and heads blew off.

The table cracked and dented with bullets. Rifle rounds slammed into the reaching hands of the swarm, tearing them off.

But still they came.

They won't stop.

Panic rose up Tealson's throat, threatening to scream out.

He choked it down.

They won't stop.

A woman, tentacles sprouting from her belly, flopped over the table as if shoved from the other side. She landed on her head, and her neck cracked, craning backward. She stood, chest forward and head looking sideways as she rushed them. She grabbed Jeff Regal, and he screamed as she yanked him toward their line.

Tealson stepped up close, aimed his XTU, and fired the last of his oversized buckshot. The rifle rocked in his hand from the blast, assuredly impossible for anyone to wield without CAG. The load blew her into red mist and crashed into Regal's arm.

Regal screamed—some of the buckshot must have gotten through—but Parker yanked him back toward the line.

A one-armed man leapt impossibly far over the line and grabbed Regal's heel.

Tealson closed in, holding the rifle high as he unloaded, splattering red pits all over the creature. Regal kicked it and the arm broke, snapping back.

But it had slowed his escape.

Regal was being crushed by a moving pile of flesh. There must've been three or more creatures, but it was no longer possible to tell where one began and the other ended.

"Help him!" Tealson screamed as they pulled him back.

The flood welled up around Regal, and they heard his screams as he was dragged away. Colton Parker yelled and reached for him, but was yanked back by other crewmen.

Regal was lost.

Dozens of hands reached in and got beneath the grooves of Regal's CAG, even as rifle fire pelted them. Their tentacles squeezed in between the plates and popped them up.

Regal's screams were lost in the sea of noise as the metal pieces broke and came off. Tealson saw a shoulder plate crack off with a sharp edge. It dragged across Jeff's arm, tearing through the skinsuit and cutting him deeply as they peeled it off. Their faces and hands found any flesh, tearing it apart as they dragged him into the maw of the swarm.

As Regal disappeared, Teaslon had a terrible realization that it was going to take them time to pry him out of the CAG. It was not going to be fast.

Regal was going to watch it happen slowly.

Tealson fired until his rifle ran dry. Then, with muscle memory that had awoken after decades of being dormant, he quickly ejected the clip and slammed another in.

But he knew they were fighting a losing battle. He knew the swarm would overtake them.

And they would all die just as Regal would.

We'll die here. We're all going to die here.

Tealson felt everything slow. His heart seemed to beat like a ticking clock and not the jackhammer it was moments ago. He was the commander. This was his squad.

They lived and died by his orders—his decisions—and it was up to him to make sure he kept them alive.

No matter the costs.

He looked back and saw they were each fighting, each waiting for an order.

Each loyal to duty.

Joseph DalBon's face was lit up in flashes of rifle fire as he screamed and fired indiscriminately into the horde. Cameron Elliot's eyes were wide and terrified, but his XTU was pumping rounds into a man on the ground threatening to stand once more.

Colton Parker, a thick and strong man, kicked a man's head off like it was a soccer ball, sending it smashing into the back wall with a sick squelching sound. Peter Becks fired his oversized buckshot, shredding four of the things into a pile of sludge. Yui Tanaka was firing at something climbing across the ceiling.

They swarm us, and even the CAGs won't last.

Something landed hard on the ground in front of him. It had

jumped from the ceiling. It wasn't one of those former men, but something else entirely.

Alien.

It was the color of a long-dead corpse. Nothing about it could be mistaken for human. It had six legs, four of which ended in sharp points and two in the front that doubled as arms, with two curling claws to walk on. Its mouth was wide, and when it shrieked, Tealson saw at least three rows of teeth.

One of these killed Pax.

That wasn't a thought so much as a reaction. Tealson stumbled back, the horror of it all so jarring it made his knees weak.

The thing had no such problems.

It jolted forward and speared its leg into Tealson's ankle. Though the CAG held, the force knocked his feet out from under him and made him slam face-first into the water. Looking through the visor with his headlamp, Tealson saw the pointed legs clicking through the water as it got closer.

The creature yanked him up into the air with ease and bit down on his armor.

Red alerts flashed in his helmet from the impact of its bite, and Tealson felt the pressure but none of the pain.

All it needed was to find a weak joint and start peeling.

"You want some, *motherfucker?*" DalBon yelled as he came close, firing his rifle and pelting Tealson and the creature.

Black blossoms of blood bloomed on its corpse-toned hide, but if it was hurt, or damaged, it wasn't clear to Tealson.

Tealson struggled with it, fighting with its powerful legs as his rifle swung by its strap around to his back.

It shrieked again and bit down, taking all of Tealson's helmet in its mouth. His lamp light shined down its throat, and Tealson saw three tongues lick up and slide over his visor, leaving a slimy trail. The glass of his helmet cracked, and the red alerts got more urgent.

Tealson reached back and grabbed his rifle. He drew it forward and blindly shoved it into the creature's chest.

He pulled the trigger.

The rifle rocked in his grasp, and the creature shook and jolted, twisting Tealson's neck so hard he thought it might crack and paralyze him.

Roaring with adrenaline, Tealson craned his head back, the creature's teeth scraping grooves across his glass visor.

"*Fuck you!*" he screamed, and now that he could see, he jammed the rifle muzzle into the soft joint of its armpit and squeezed the trigger.

The creature thrashed, and speckles of black blood splattered Tealson's face. It jammed a pointed claw into his stomach, knocking the wind out of him.

Oozing blood from the pit of its arm, the creature had taken enough. It slung him away, and he crashed into the back wall, looking up to see the swarm of once-men darting right around the creature.

"Come on, get up!" Becks grabbed Tealson under the arm and hefted him to his feet.

In a daze, Tealson looked across his crew. They were all standing their ground. They were all fighting for their lives. Each was in the moment, a slave to violence and self-preservation.

The line had been overrun. This was not a fight they could win.

They were all going to die.

Think.

Tealson told himself in between heartbeats.

The cut in the door is too small.

A thin man-thing came close to him. Tealson kicked it back with the power of the CAG, and it flew back into the crowd.

We'd get bottled up, and only a few would make it back.

"Fuck you! Fuck you!" Becks screamed over and over as he fired into a once-woman that had closed in on them, making her dance from the impact.

Make a plan now, or you're all dead.

Tealson glanced back once more and saw a door—the kitchen entrance from the cafeteria.

There.

"Fall back!" Tealson screamed, waving toward the door. "Back to the kitchen! Get back!" He turned and fired, then looked to see someone had rushed to the kitchen already and pushed the door open. The others also broke rank and started running.

The swarm flowed like an incoming tidal wave the moment the rifle fire stopped. Those on the ground clawed through the water and were quickly trampled by the others with functioning legs.

It was hard to see who was breaking and who was running.

Tealson let off another burst and ran to the door. He huffed in panic as he saw the last of his team to go inside. His lungs burned as he ran, afraid they would close the door and leave him on the other side.

Something grabbed his shoulder, slowing his escape. He turned to see a long arm where the meat and muscle had decayed. It shouldn't have had any control at all, but beneath the blinking emergency lights and his head lamp, he saw the thick tentacles coiled around it, giving it strength, having surely fed from the host's own tissue to survive.

In a rage, Tealson snapped his hand back, hard enough that it broke clean through the elbow and snapped the arm off.

The creature hissed, but its arm still clung to Tealson as he hurtled through the doorway.

Elliot slammed the door shut. Parker twisted the lock, and the others started piling equipment in front of it. Tealson peeled the clawed arm off his CAG and threw it aside. He tossed his rifle onto a counter and helped overturn a table, making dishes and silverware crash into the water below. They shoved it in front of the door.

The things beat on the door, but it didn't budge. The creatures screamed and raged on the other side.

"Fuck me," Elliot said, pacing the room. He tossed his rifle onto a table and clasped his hands behind his neck. *"Fuck me."*

"A hundred and fifty?" Becks said, pacing and screaming. "There's more than a goddamn hundred and fifty! Ain't no one alive on this piece of shit station! No one!"

Parker had slumped into a chair, and now stared down at the floor awkwardly and confused. "They don't die. They just keep getting up."

Tealson huffed, finding it hard to breathe. The reality of the situation was quickly becoming apparent.

There was no victory here. No way to fight back a screaming horde.

We're trapped.

They might be able to take them a few at the time, but the things on the other side of the door, still screaming, could just—

"*Wait*," DalBon said, looking around the room. "Where's Tanaka?"

Tealson tensed up, coming off the wall. He hadn't even realized he'd slumped against it.

"Where the hell is Tanaka?" DalBon's eyes were wide and panicking. Everyone in the room went deadly silent.

And somehow, in the crowd of painful screams and tortured sounds, Tealson was certain he could hear Tanaka screaming.

Can't help her.

"She's out there!" DalBon yelled, looking among all of them.

Can't help anyone.

Becks shook his head, tears rolling down his eyes. "Nothing we can do for her, man."

"We gotta get her!" DalBon said, not hearing Becks. He threw his rifle strap over his shoulder and grabbed the equipment piled in front of the door, trying to move it. "Help me!" he screamed back at the others, but they didn't move. "Get off your fucking asses, and *help me*!"

Tealson couldn't speak. His left eye and cheek twitched.

Was it fear? Cowardice?

. . . or just horrible self-loathing?

You did this.

"We can't help her!" Elliot screamed in a spitting rage. "She's dead! Fuck her!"

You made them come.

"Fuck you!" DalBon's eyes lit with an anger Tealson had never seen. "You piece of shit coward!" He looked over at Tealson and yelled again. "We have to help her!"

It hurt. From the deepest part of his soul, the pain seeped from his eyes. It hurt.

You did this.

Tealson shook his head. It was all he could do.

"You fucking pussy!" DalBon pointed at Tealson and then looked around the room and screamed as loudly as he could. *"You worthless, goddamn cowards!"*

"She's already dead." Becks slumped down. "We're *all* already dead."

DalBon turned and kicked an oven hard enough to put a hole in it. He bellowed out in rage and hammered his fist against it. They all watched him silently. "You pieces of shit," DalBon muttered as he calmed down. He leaned forward and put his hand against a wall, looking as if he might throw up. "You're all worthless *cowards. . ."*

No one voiced their disagreement.

7

We heard a knock.

Had Braun been so eager before? So naive to illusion and subterfuge?

We heard a knock.

The voice of Mark Rufus, a dead and decaying man, echoed in his mind with regular annoyance. He'd been a colleague—possibly even the closest thing Braun had to a friend on Felicity.

Hadn't there been a spark of caution? A moment of doubt amongst them that begged the question: *Maybe we shouldn't answer the unknown? Maybe it's Hell and it wants to come inside?*

But doubt had never been part of who William Braun was. He'd known since he was a little boy that he didn't act like others. He didn't *think* like others.

He wasn't like others.

The world turns no matter how much hurt there is. And, in time, all pain is forgotten, and only progress remains. He knew this, deep within the marrow of his bones. He'd always understood that.

Sacrifices can be made.

They *should* be made.

What was one small group of people to the evolution of a culture? What cost could be measured when the benefits were so great?

Endless.

That had been the reward for their risk.

None amongst them—including Braun—had imagined what *could* happen, but they'd all had their theories.

The Russians had new oil veins seemingly every day, and Braun had read about a new discovery of rare Earth metals only a week before the *incident* here on Felicity.

What if there had been a knock, and a door was opened? What if resources beyond imagination were inside, and Braun had been able to take them?

The war would have been won.

There would be other, endless possibilities. World hunger, poverty, technological advancement—the potential to change mankind's entire history was at their fingertips.

He was the point upon which fate turned.

So now, in contemplation and reflection of his actions, Braun saw that, no, he hadn't acted recklessly, and no, he did not need to concern himself with the failures of the past, but instead with only the potential of the future.

So now he sat in their small, secure room, hunched down and thinking. His gaze clicked back and forth like a pendulum in a clock.

Tick. Tick. Tick.

He was counting moments. He was counting lives. And he was predicting courses of action.

Thirty-five percent survival predictability. Unacceptable.

Another plan formed in his head, as he willed the gears of his mind to turn faster. Dixie had been confident she'd overloaded the gate, but each wasted moment was one more second for it to return.

He did not intend to waste the advantage. Dixie had bought it with her blood.

"What are we going to do?" someone asked him. It had gone past the point of annoying and into the territory of hysterically amusing that they would keep asking him even though he never answered them.

Hysterically amusing, yes, but still, he didn't laugh.

Braun was not a man who laughed.

A course through Felicity lit up in his mind. The odds began calculating, considering the particulars of where the creatures originated from, the size of the hallways and the ease in which they could travel them, and the creatures' hunting patterns.

And that he was sure now they were climbing through the internals of the base.

Dixie had been proof of that.

Eighty-seven percent survival predictability. This is acceptable.

"We're leaving," Braun said as he got to his feet. He turned to the survivors. They were mewling and trembling like beaten dogs. For a moment, Braun wondered what it was like to be so afraid, to be so certain of your mortality...

The moment passed.

"We need to get past the epicenter of the gate room," he said. "We'll have to take an indirect route to avoid the most likely chances of engagement."

"How about through the cafeteria?" a thin man asked, his face wet and waxy. "We could cut through there and get to the docking bay right away."

"No," Braun said flatly, a scratch of irritation rising up his throat for needing to restate. "We will travel *indirectly*. The cafeteria was a bloodbath before. I saw them as they fell on the crowd there. Come with me now. Be quiet, and be quick."

Braun was not an inspiring leader. He knew and understood that *inspiration* was not a skill he possessed. If they followed, it would be because they were afraid.

This, he understood.

And then, as if by divine intervention, the lights blinked and came on. Long dormant machines suddenly hummed to life.

"The lights are back on," Braun said as if this should bring them some comfort.

"Is that really good though?" the thin man asked. "Won't it be harder for us to hide?"

"I saw a man I recognized before," Braun said as he turned to face him. "It was a bit difficult as he had no head at all, but he often wore the same stupid sweater vest. He must have been wearing that sweater vest when something ate his head. Either way, the loss of the head seemed no real disadvantage to him when it came to moving about."

"Oh my—"

"And the creatures, the ones from another world?" Braun frowned. "They don't have eyes at all." He looked around to the others. "I suppose the lights will only do us good then, yes?"

No one remarked or moved.

"I'm leaving. Stay or go, it is your choice." Braun went to the door and slid away the desk and chairs the idiots had piled up in front of it. The group came to help him, and he worked the commands. The door slid into the wall, and the water began to flow in instantly.

The shutters were rising, and the sun was coming in. Lights glowed overhead, though some flickered occasionally.

"That's certainly better," Braun said as he stepped out. "Now, if only we could do something about this damn water."

THEY'D MADE a loop around the facility, staying close to the outer edge and near the windows. Braun appreciated the sight of Mars, even if it was cold and dead.

He found it comforting.

Braun walked upright and unafraid, his hand sliding on the wall's guard rail for extra support as they sloshed through the water. Occasionally, he would stop and listen, holding his hand up for the others to do the same. Each time he heard only the mumbles of the others and the faint clicking of his own internal mechanics.

"Braun," someone whispered behind him. "*Braun.*"

Frowning, he looked back. "*What?*"

It was a woman in glasses. She pushed them up on her nose. "I have to pee."

A larger man huffed and held the guard rail. "And I need some goddamn food, or I'm going to pass out."

Braun shook his head. "We passed the living quarters already. These labs won't have any food."

"My lab." She stopped to take a breath and pointed just down the hall. "It's right up there. There's a bathroom inside, and I have some things we can eat."

Reluctantly, Braun nodded. "Fine."

They trudged to the door, and the woman leaned in close, opening her eyes wide. "*Access*," she said as it scanned her face.

The red door light flipped green.

It had clearly been sealed since everything happened, and the water rushed in as the door slid into the wall. They all got inside, and it closed again.

"Go rest, we'll leave here in fifteen minutes," Braun said. He stayed close to the entrance, peering through a window to admire Mars.

The group was talking and eating crackers they'd salvaged from the desk. The woman even came and offered Braun a handful. "Here, you should eat too."

Braun accepted them without a word and started eating, never taking his eyes from the window.

Despite all that had happened, Braun still enjoyed the view. He hoped that one day this base would be reestablished, with necessary precautions, of course.

His research was crucial for the war effort, and there was still much work to do.

He was only one man, though. The growling in his stomach as he began to eat reminded him of that. It was as if he hadn't known he was hungry until he started eating, and with that, he began to feel tired and drained.

This was why he didn't like the work to pause, why it was foolish to take any break when there was more work to be done. Flesh fails the moment it is given a chance. Braun always ran a tight crew, and they would work hard until late into the night and retire only after—

"Braun?" the woman with the crackers asked.

Deep in thought, Braun had almost forgotten she was there. He didn't answer but only looked at her, blinking hard in hopes of stopping one of his eyes from malfunctioning.

"I have an idea." She brushed a strand of hair behind her ear. "There's an airlock in my office."

He frowned, but still said nothing.

"It was for quick cargo loading. We were developing—"

"What *about* the airlock?" Braun finally spoke.

"Come here." She motioned him to follow and led him to the back of her office and then into another room.

There were robotic arms and long-dead plants inside of airtight cases. Bags of soil were stacked up in containers, giving the room an earthy smell. The roof was entirely glass, presumably to allow light for whatever botany experiments were being performed. In the back, there was a large, half-circle glass door—an airlock. It had two doors securing it from the outside.

"I think we could use this." She gestured. "If we were able to get the correct equipment, we could head out the airlock and then just round the base and go to the bay. We could avoid the threats altogether."

"Do you have any all-atmosphere suits?" Braun asked, raising an eyebrow.

"No, but I—"

"Do you know where they are located?"

She shook her head.

"They are located near the bay, where we are going, and thus useless for the purposes you have described." Braun felt his brain itching.

"I was just saying that we could potentially use it if we had the proper equipment."

"Yes. If we had the proper equipment, then a stroll across Mars is really no problem at all. However, we do not. Would you advise us to walk across Mars and just hold our breath?"

"You're such an asshole..."

There was a scream.

Braun turned away from her and froze in place.

The scream continued. The long, painful gasps and shrieks sounded entirely human and nothing like the moaning creatures.

Braun stepped into the main room and could see out the window. All he saw was the landscape of Mars through the window on the other side of the hallway.

The others were talking and whispering amongst themselves, but Braun quickly went to the control pad on the window and clicked a few keys. The entire window darkened so that anyone in the hallway couldn't see into the lab. Without looking away from the window, he pointed at the door. "Close and lock the door, please."

Someone rushed up and pressed the commands, and the door quickly closed and locked. Braun was pressing his face close to the glass, looking for the monsters.

As the door locked and sealed, they could no longer hear anything from the outside. Braun waited.

He leaned forward and looked down the hallway, and in time, the diseased and dying former colleagues of Braun's ambled into his hallway, passing his way.

"*Hmm*," Braun mumbled under his breath as they filtered in.

More and more came into view. Each looked broken and torn apart, as if they'd just escaped a fight.

"I hope they didn't just kill our rescue team," he said with a rare display of his dark humor.

Some of the men lacked arms and heads, but each had hideous, insectile features. One with a broken, three-jointed leg erupting from its back led the pack. It's long leg stretched toward the windows and dragged a deep scratch across the glass, sending a chill down Braun's spine.

Another creature moaned and gagged, though Braun couldn't hear it. Without slowing her walk, she tilted her head back. The skin split across her forehead, and a tentacle stretched out as if giving birth. It looked raw and chewed, but bent and squirmed as if searching.

Braun clicked a button on the window and the sounds from outside activated, though they were quited.

There were screams—*human screams*—and Braun had to press his face closer to the glass to see what was making them.

The creatures dragged a woman into view. She was in full combat armor, but they had somehow managed to pry her helmet off and at least part of her armored sleeve.

Very much alive, she screamed and thrashed as they dragged her right in front of the lab door. He twisted his head to follow her. She was an Asian woman and still fairly young. Her face was twisted with emotions of horror. Strangely, she appeared not to be infected.

Interesting.

They stayed clustered with her, enough arms and tentacles latched about her to keep her from moving much.

Another creature—one that had clearly come through the gate—prowled alongside the Asian woman. It hissed and raised its lips in ever-present hostility. It too moved in front of Braun's window behind the crowd of once-men.

Then it stopped.

And slowly, it twisted its head in Braun's direction.

If Braun had a heart, it might have stopped. Instinct and panic rose through him and made him want to turn or fall back.

But he was not a slave to fear.

With startling speed, it jolted toward the window and pressed its face close. The window was strong, but Braun doubted it could hold if the beast desired to break through it.

Behind him, Braun heard the group gasp, and that bout of weakness inside them surely would have given everyone away.

That irrational weakness was still there in Braun, still clawing at him to pull back and to hide. As if hiding in a corner might prolong his life if the creature came in. Perhaps it wouldn't kill him. Maybe they would just take him like the screaming woman.

They would drag him away and feed him to the same thing they were taking the woman to. He was sure that was what they were doing, and there wouldn't be anything he could do about it. Living his last moments in fear would not save him.

So he leaned forward into the glass—into the face of the monster—to challenge the anxiety inside of himself.

Emotion was not a thing to submit to, but to conquer.

But still, there was a struggle raging within him.

Did it suspect they were here? Could its hearing be so acute that it actually *heard* them?

Though it had no eyes, it appeared to look across the window, ambling from side to side and inspecting the corners of the glass.

Braun held a hand up to his side, demanding total silence from the rest of the group. He narrowed his own gaze as he watched it, barely catching his reflection in the glass.

A slit opened on the skin of its back, as if it was unzipping. The flesh was thick on both sides but not bleeding. A pointed claw poked out and then emerged—impossibly long—and Braun noted it must have had the bony leg folded beneath its flesh.

They were bizarre and unique creatures.

Fascinating.

"*Oh fuck,*" someone whispered.

Slowly, Braun turned and held a finger to his lips. He then looked back.

The creature reached a two-fingered hand up to the glass and pressed on it. Leaning forward, its face waved back and forth like a snake.

Braun noticed that it was not fogging the window.

It's not breathing.

He knew they were something he couldn't understand, not in the present moment. Like explaining colors to a man born blind—it was impossible, *at the moment.* He would come to understand them. He would come to learn how a creature sees with no eyes and lives without breathing. How a leg could fold inside, and how a bite could turn people into slaves.

They were merely questions awaiting answers.

It pulled back, stepping backward but keeping its face in the reflection.

Braun had seen that move before. Animals did it.

It usually meant they were about to pounce.

But that wasn't going to happen, because if it did, Braun would then be in a small, locked room with it. Everything would happen too fast, and he wouldn't be able to unlock the door. It would only ravage him, perhaps with a single attack, and then kill everyone else.

And Braun would die stupidly.

That wasn't going to happen.

It lowered its back, its front shoulder muscles engaging.

But it wasn't going to jump.

That wouldn't happen.

The creature knew it too, perhaps in some primitive, less-evolved portion of its brain. That's why it froze in place, holding tight with coiled muscles but not yet jumping. It knew it was trying to break the rules of fate. It had no mind. No real choice. This was fate, once more, trying to provoke him, trying to get him to blink or show fear. It was a joke.

A gnawing itch surfaced on the right side of Braun's temple, one of the few places of flesh left on his body. Some might have called it fear, or the beginning of panic, but not Braun. He was not afraid. He was only intently watching and waiting for the joke to end.

It didn't.

The creature sprang forth and burst through the glass, and Braun moved faster than an old man with more metal than bones had any right to. Broken glass rained on him, but he held an arm up to block it from getting in his eyes.

When he opened his eyes again, he saw it killing the thin man.

It had speared him through the belly, and blood was pouring through his mouth. It tossed the body aside and looked across the room as the others panicked. The creature was between them and Braun, and they rushed into the backroom.

Braun's mind worked at blazing speed.

Door? Dead? Yes. Locked. Time to unlock too long.

Broken window? Dead? Yes. Glass shards snag. Held in place. Killed while caught.

Move to backroom? Dead? No. Go. Now.

Braun rushed toward the backroom and saw everyone there, cowering. A bald man took up hiding behind a large piece of equipment. The botanist was cowering between stacks of fertilizer. The rest had equally terrible ideas.

But one man had made it inside the airlock. He frantically typed on the keypad to close the door between the airlock and the lab.

Braun headed toward it and hit the keys inside the lab, overriding the man's commands.

"What are you doing, Braun?" the man said on the other side as the doors stopped closing and began to open again. "Get in fast, and close it!"

Braun didn't look at him. He only glanced backward, half anticipating, half *feeling* the sharp point of its leg piercing his chest.

"Hurry, Braun! Get inside! It's getting—"

Braun heard nothing else. His focus was on the creature, slowly, painfully walking into the room with them.

Taking its time.

It wanted to kill him. It wanted to break his bones and eat his flesh.

But it wasn't going to.

This is a joke.

It arched down, and its shoulder muscles coiled.

A particularly funny one.

It leapt, and Braun moved, allowing the thing to collide with the man inside.

He screamed and thrashed as Braun's back stiffened. He reached out and hit the buttons. The door rose, more slowly than Braun would've liked, but the creature stayed distracted with the man.

As the door closed, the man's screams became silent to those on the other side of the wall. Braun watched from behind the safety of the thick, reinforced glass as the creature opened up the man's abdomen and uncoiled his organs across the floor.

It was silent now, and the man, still living, might have been cursing Braun as the creature stopped its assault to cautiously move about the locked room. Braun clicked a few buttons to command the airlock to open to Mars.

The creature backed away cautiously as the door rose. It then bit a strand of the man's intestines and dragged him off to the surface of the cold, red planet.

Braun watched as the man thrashed from the new atmosphere. The creature looked only momentarily panicked before attacking him again, as it was clearly unaffected by being on Mars' surface.

Interesting.

Braun worked the commands to close the outer door and open the inner door once more. There was now a noticeable puddle of blood. The others crept from their hiding places, all cautious and breathing heavily.

Still watching the creature outside of Felicity, Braun said to no one in particular, "Go gather the dead man from the other room." Braun intently watched the creature attack the man once more before he remembered to be polite. "Please."

A woman with short-cropped, brown hair swallowed short breaths of air. "But... Dr. Conners is still alive."

"Oh, I see, " Braun said, his voice a single, unfluctuating tone. "Place him in the airlock."

8

THE KITCHEN HAD BEEN a death trap. They'd searched the room and had come up empty. The only exit was the one through which they'd entered. The situation became all the more depressing when the lights came back on, and Tealson could see just how low everyone's shoulders sagged.

Parker still sat in his chair, elbows propped on the table in front of him. "What are they, though? Why would . . ." He trailed off as his eyes searched the empty table for an answer. "Why would anything do that?"

Tealson had barely heard him because he wasn't there. He wasn't in that moment.

He was twenty minutes back, and he was dying before the door closed.

Because that's what he wanted.

Dead. He wanted to be dead.

"We're going to die here. Earth Command fucked us. They *fucked* us," Elliot said, the sound of defeat thick in his voice. He looked up at Tealson and shook his head. "We need to call Winters's group. Get them to come up here." He nodded nervously. "Get them up here, and we can attack from all sides."

"Get them killed, you mean," DalBon scoffed. He hadn't said much since he'd slumped down to the floor in the shin-deep water. "More bodies for the brush fire."

"No, *no*," Elliot said frantically. He laughed as if DalBon was making another one of his jokes. "We're not dead. We just need them to help us. That's all we need, we just... We just need some help."

Becks was busily going through the cupboards, carelessly knocking things to the floor.

They were all cracking. All coming apart at the seams, and why was that?

Because of you.

Tealson brought them here. He forced them down and led them right into the maw, and he didn't even have the good grace to die when the plan went to hell.

An annoying bead of sweat rolled down Tealson's face, and he was unable to wipe it in the thick, helmeted CAG.

You led them here. Right off the ship. Straight into the cafeteria, and then into the kitchen. All because some asshole back on earth told you to.

Everyone dies because of you.

His heart pounded in his chest in fast, heavy beats, and he could swear he felt the blood oozing through his veins. He wished it would just stop. That he could just have a heart attack and die, because he couldn't look any of them in the eye. All any of them would have to say was *You left Tanaka out there* and he'd shoot himself right here and now. Paint the whole wall a nice shade of *brains* red.

He hadn't left her outside because of fear. Not for himself anyway. He'd done it because he had to make a choice. Cut the finger to save the hand. He continued to silently make the wish that it had been him out there and Tanaka in here. He'd make that trade in a moment.

He kept wishing it. Over and over again. As if he could reach into the past and exchange his life for Tanaka's. He prayed for it. Prayed that God would kill him and not her. And if not, then for God to reach into his chest and squeeze his heart right now so he could—

"*Hey*," Becks said. His eyes were wide and curious. "I think I found something?"

It was a struggle for Tealson to speak when all he wanted to do was die. "What?" he croaked, still flat on his ass on the floor, his back to the wall.

"See this?" Becks pointed to something beneath the grill. "Come here."

The others looked up, but no one moved.

"*Come here*," Becks insisted, gesturing to Tealson.

Tealson struggled to his feet and moved to the cupboard. He looked in, the light on his helmet shining across the tanks of fuel beneath the grill.

"They got external fuel cells here." He grinned like a maniac and pointed to one of the largest tanks. Its gauge read it three-quarters full. "This goddamn place. It's so old. It's not even a modern set up. This is pure—"

"So what?" Elliot huffed. "We can blow something up? What do you want to do, open the door and—"

"You're goddamn right that's what I want to do!" Becks shouted and pointed a finger at Elliot. "You dipshits are sitting around crying." He slapped his hand on his chest. "I don't want to *fucking* die here."

Here's your chance.

Elliot opened his mouth to say something, but Tealson held up his hand. "*Shut up.*"

Tanaka and Regal died so they could live. So you could live.

What a joke.

Tealson was quiet for a moment, thinking.

Do it. Save them. Kill yourself after if you want, but save them.

"He's right," Tealson said. "Can you remove the tank without it leaking?"

Becks nodded his head. "Think so."

"Here's what we're going to do," Tealson said. "We're going to get that out and put it right in front of the door. Then I'll—"

"Let them in?" Elliot's eyes were wide. "We're going to let them in?"

"You'd rather us just starve to death?" DalBon said as he climbed to his feet. "Besides, I need to take a piss in the worst way." He looked pale and clammy, but he'd found his composure again. He nodded to Tealson and snatched up his rifle.

Tealson went on, "I'm going to open the door. As they start to pour in, Becks is going to fire on the tanks and blow them into pieces."

"What happens if they don't die?" Parker asked, his face still frowning in confusion.

"Then we mop up whatever is left because we're out of options." Tealson glanced over at Elliot. "Unless you care to enlighten us with a better idea?"

Elliot took a deep breath, he held it, and then sighed. "I don't have shit. You're right."

"I'm going to radio Winters's group, let them know what we're doing," Tealson said as he pressed the button.

"This is Tealson. Winters, do you read?"

Static sizzled and popped.

"Winters? Reeves? Anyone? Do you read?" Tealson idly glanced around the room.

"Communication is still fucked." DalBon bit his bottom lip irritably.

"They might be getting something," Tealson said and pushed the comms button again.

"This is Tealson. We were overrun in the cafeteria and were forced to retreat to the kitchen. Repeat, we were *overrun*. We're now going to make the attempt to fight our way out. We're blowing a fuel tank. Repeat, we will *blow a fuel tank*. Advise you to proceed with caution." He thought for a moment before pressing the button once more. "Be careful."

Tealson let go of the button and all the men turned to look at him. He pointed at Peter. "Get it ready."

9

"Come on!" Alice reached down for Smith, grabbing him by the wrists. With the added strength of her CAG, she was able to pull him up fairly easily. With his wounded arm, he was struggling to get up the ladder.

They'd rebooted the power, but it had been a constant fight for their lives.

Down beneath the hatch, there were sounds of gunfire and sporadic flashes of light.

"*Fuck off!*" someone below cursed between blasts.

With Smith dragged out, Alice reached down for the next.

"Get out of my way!" Bartlet shoved her hand away as he climbed out.

Alice ignored him and looked down to see Tommy hurrying up the ladder.

"Come on!" she yelled and shoved her hand down toward him.

Tommy got his arm out and threw his gun through. He grabbed Alice's hand, and she yanked him the rest of the way up.

"Close it! Close the goddamn thing!" Bartlet roared as he grabbed the hatch and grunted. Tommy yanked his legs out even as Bartlet was shoving the hatch over. It slammed into place with a loud bang. Both

Bartlet and Tommy got on the crank, and the old metal groaned as it tightened into place.

Below, the creatures scratched at the door. They screamed, though the sound was muffled. Even so, Alice could feel her chest tightening.

I can't breathe...

"Go to Hell!" Bartlet gave the finger to the closed hatch.

Now that they were up, a switch seemed to flip somewhere within Alice. She took two wobbly steps backward and held her hand to her helmet, smearing blood across her visor.

In a haze, she looked at the blood, confused by where it had come from, or who it belonged to.

This was a dream. She was sure of it now. As sure as she was that when you blow a man's head off, he dies.

But when she wiped the blood off her helmet, she saw Smith cradling his arm and leaning against the wall.

He was screaming, but the words weren't making sense to her.

Tommy came close to Smith and leaned down to inspect his arm. He was talking, but the words still made no sense to her.

When she breathed, it was loud and ragged. She wasn't getting enough air, even with the CAG feeding it to her. It was like sucking through a straw. She felt as if she could crumple to the floor now and let the dream go on until she woke up.

She could fall right into the void.

It was all hitting her now. Libya. Fall of Tripoli. The nightmare that broke her. The nightmare that made her crawl to her father.

"Dad," she'd said, tears already steaming down her face. She never called him dad anymore, she'd called him John since the last time they fought.

John Winters. That was who he was. He was the one that told her she was strong. That told her she could do anything. Be anything.

As long as it fit his plan. His vision.

"*Can you get me out of here, Dad?*" she had squeaked out the words. Her eyes were nearly drawn shut, and her teeth chattered. They were going to send them back out again, and she hadn't yet gotten the dirt and blood out from under her fingernails.

"I don't..." She'd been so pathetic. So childish.

So weak.

Her fingers had curled around the phone. She'd slid down the wall and tightened into a ball. Her chest barely drew in enough air to speak. *"I don't want to be here anymore."*

But she wasn't in Tripoli.

She was on Mars.

And John Winters wasn't here.

Bartlet came around her now, rifle in hand and pointing a finger at Smith. Tommy straightened up, and they argued.

There were words. She heard them, but they just didn't click. She'd felt as if she'd been in a car wreck. Her brain slammed into the present moment.

Bartlet raised his rifle, and Tommy stepped in, shoving him. Bartlet shoved back, and now they were yelling.

"What?" Alice said to no one, and no one answered. She swallowed again, trying to drag focus together. *"What?"*

"—kill him!" Bartlet roared. "Same as Mike Burns! Fucker will—"

"Stop it," Alice said and gasped for air. "Just—"

"Not your call, asshole!" Tommy came close pointing a finger at Bartlet's head. "You don't get to—"

"It hurts!" Smith wailed. *"Fuck me, it hurts."* He gritted his teeth.

"He's fucked." Bartlet's eyes were wide, but now he stepped back.

"Shut up," Alice straightened her back. Her rifle had gone loose on its strap, so she slid it back in front of her. "Shut *up*," she said through gritted teeth.

"Going to kill us!" Bartlet pointed a finger at Smith. Bartlet was shouting, but he wasn't angry.

He's afraid.

"Smith?" Alice staggered between Bartlet and Tommy and leaned down to Smith. "Is it in your arm? Can you feel it?"

Laughing painfully, he nodded his head. "I can feel the little shit moving around."

"Med lab." She leaned up, her head still woozy. "We need to get him to the med lab."

"And do *what?*" Bartlet shouted. "Just leave him here. It's nothing personal, Smith." Bartlet was breathing hard. "I'm sorry, but we have to—"

"Fuck you! How's that for personal?" Smith licked his lips and looked back at Alice. "You can put me in cryo, can't you?" He nodded frantically. "Just get me on the ship and put me in goddamn cryo. Let me sleep until we're back on Earth. Someone will know what to—"

"You saw what happened to Mike!" Bartlet shouted. "There's no choice!" He looked between Alice and Tommy. "We need to plug him right here. I'd want the same for me. It's not—"

"Shut up!" Alice shouted. "Shut the fuck up!" Alice stood up and thumbed at her chest. "I'm in charge here, so *shut up!*"

Bartlet opened his mouth to say something, but Tommy shoved between them. "She told you to shut your damn mouth, Bartlet!" He looked at Alice. "Can you save him?" she nodded. "*Can you?*" Tommy asked again more forcefully.

"*Yes,*" she said with as much force as she could muster. "But we're not going to the ship." Smith was terrified, his eyes gaping wide and sweating so bad he looked as though he was melting. But she insisted, "I'm sorry, but we can't risk it. But I know what we're dealing with now, we have to get to the med lab, fast, and I can take it out of you."

"Then—" Smith shook his head, blinking hard. "Then quit talking, and let's move!"

"*Fine,*" Bartlet spat. His face had turned a pale white. "As long we're not going any farther in."

The comm system burst to life with static and fragments too unintelligible to understand.

"The damn signal is still shit." Tommy shook his head at them. He pressed a button, activating his comm. "This is Reeves. We cannot read you. Repeat, we cannot read you. Say again."

The static burst once more. "*—overrun—attempt to—way out—*" it sizzled. *—blowing a fuel—with caution—*" it fizzled out.

"*Shit,*" Tommy hissed.

"Huh? The hell did any of that mean?" Bartlet asked.

Tommy snatched his rifle off the ground. "*Hell*, I'm not sure, but it sounds like they're going to blow something up."

Bartlet shrugged as if to deny any reason for concern. "I heard Bennie running his mouth. This whole damn base was built to withstand a missile from the Russians."

"Not from the inside." Tommy waved his hand at the water. "This whole thing is compromised and was renovated so many times that no one knows where half the shit is. They blow one bad spot and we'll decompress or pop a cryo tank."

"Keeps getting *fucking* better, doesn't it?" Bartlet leaned up, shaking his head.

Tommy looked at Alice, and she knew what he was going to say before he said it. She could read his face.

Every part of her wanted to tell him to stay where he was, but she knew that wasn't how he worked.

"Be fast," was all she said.

Tommy nodded. "You know how to get to the med lab from here?"

Alice nodded. "You don't worry about us. You just watch your own ass, Reeves."

Tommy looked at Bartlet. "You give her any shit. . . " He left the threat at that.

"All right!" Smith moaned. "Let's get our asses moving."

Alice gave Tommy one last look. He nodded at her, and then turned to run.

"Let's go," she said and moved with the others toward the med lab.

EVER SINCE TOMMY was a small boy, he'd gazed at the stars. It was a dream of his to go into space and look back down at the Earth, to see it as God does.

But dreams have a habit of dying as you get older.

He'd joined the Air Force because it had looked like the best route through college. It wasn't long before he'd become the hamster on a wheel that runs but doesn't get anywhere.

Running fast just to stay in one place. But that was life, wasn't it?

Marrying his college sweetheart was the first step down that path. She was beautiful, smart, and funny. And she wanted to go on living right there in the same town she'd grown up in.

That was fine.

They'd been good to each other, and Tommy would have told anyone that he loved his wife. They liked watching movies together. Though that was the only hobby they'd shared.

When he'd been transferred to Iraq, he kissed her goodbye, and they knew they'd see each other in a few months.

That was fine.

Those long stints became longer than originally expected, and that was fine. And everything else that had happened after that fateful phone call where she told him she'd moved on?

Also fine.

That had been Tommy's life from the moment he stopped looking up at the stars.

Fine. Just *fine*.

He hadn't known who he really was until the divorce. It was as if that dissolution was a wake-up call to make him understand how hollow he really was. He'd been lying to himself. He hadn't cared about anything in years.

But now, as he loaded a fresh mag into his XTU and heard the *click* as he drummed back the slide, he knew he wasn't hollow anymore.

And he knew what he cared about.

Wading through the water, Tommy moved right past an open shutter. He saw the orange landscape, the dusty, desolate terrain of this foreign planet. That was when it finally hit him. He was on Mars. The place he'd wanted to go for so long, the place he'd looked at when he stared up into the stars.

He'd made it.

And that was just fine.

But he wasn't hollow now. He had a purpose, and he had people who depended on him.

And he wasn't going to let them down.

Shuffling through the water, he saw the blinking lights of a small provisions store. It was a go-between that had been placed between two hallways to drum up business from the busy occupants of Felicity walking though several times a day. He headed through its crescent archway and saw it was run down and water-soaked, but still lined with rows and rows of junk food.

Something chirped. An alien, wheezing sound.

Tommy's blood froze cold, and he tightened up against a shelf, bending his knees and easing down toward the water. There were small gaps in the shelving, and as he leaned down, he got a view of what was making the noise.

A man, or rather, something that had once been a man, was shuffling through the water. It had its arms curled up in front of its chest, and its neck was cracked down to its shoulder. A long, wet tendril with a blinking eye had grown from a wound in its throat. The eye looked hairy, as thick bristles grew directly out of the orb.

It blinked and moved, slowly looking around.

Don't let that thing see you.

Tommy's lungs began to burn as he realized he hadn't drawn a breath.

Slowly, he sipped in air to cool the flame in his chest.

The once-man's head, wobbling against its shoulder, chirped and whined. A thing from Hell if Tommy had ever seen one.

Let it pass… Let it pass…

It kept shuffling, and Tommy turned around the corner as it came his way, getting out of sight. He pressed closer to the rack, watching through the gaps as it waded out of the provisions store.

Tommy kept his eye on it as he backpedaled toward the front of the store.

As he turned, his breath caught a second time.

There, on the counter, was a body so devoured, so broken, that it couldn't move on its own.

But still, it tried.

The blood around it had long-since dried, and its legs and arms had been chewed until there was no muscle or tissue left. A face stared up at Tommy, eyes opening and closing as its jaw worked, trying something—anything—to get at him.

It started to hiss, a gray tongue struggling to make more noise while its eyes rolled around in its head. A broken spinal column leaned up like a rising snake and jerked from left to right.

Even after all he'd seen, it still froze Tommy in place. He clenched his rifle to his chest and moved past it, keeping his focus on it.

The creature continued, moaning and hissing.

A wet hand slapped the glass near the entrance, and that's when it all finally hit Tommy.

It called for help...

The creature with the broken neck came tearing back into the convenience store. Tommy backpedaled and tripped on something beneath the water, he fell forward sending up a splash.

Submerged beneath the water, he saw a tentacle reaching up for him. An alien creature, no bigger than his forearm, was roping up his leg. The damn thing had *tripped* him.

Tommy grabbed the tentacle with both hands, letting his rifle go loose on its strap. With the added strength of his CAG, his fingers dug in, and it snapped in his grasp. Black blood leaked out, and the shrieking alien creature jetted away in the water.

Tommy came up, breaking the surface. He saw the creature with the broken neck was nearly upon him, its large eye on the stalk blinking and wet.

Scrambling to his feet, Tommy grabbed a rack of snacks and turned it over, putting it firmly between the creature and himself.

It came up to the rack and reached for Tommy, but his rifle was pointed and ready.

"Fuck off!" he yelled.

Seemingly taking the cue, the thing turned away. It then reached for the creature with the broken body.

Puzzled, Tommy looked on as it scooped up the broken creature. Each creature had small strands growing out and reaching. The wisps glided toward each other with a magnetic-like pull. The standing creature placed the broken one on top of itself. Tommy watched in horror as they merged.

Two heads on one body.

Why in the hell would it do that?

Tommy only had a moment to ask that question before broken flaps of skin and meat swung around the creature's arm, making it thicker and heavier than before. It reached down and tossed the rack aside.

Tommy had seen enough. He brought his rifle up and unloaded a blast. Concerns about the sound of gunfire be damned.

The impact of the bullets created black blossoms of decayed blood across the thing's rotten body. It jerked and reached its arm back, hurling itself forward as its broken body collided with Tommy.

The monstrosity slapped against him and curled its one good arm around his waist. Its moaning face pressed close to his helmet.

The parasitic strands crawled from it, reaching and terrible. While the flesh was weak and rotten, the wisps were thin and colorless. They squirmed out of the body and wrapped around Tommy's forearm. They were thin but incredibly strong.

"Get off me!" Tommy screamed as he jerked away. It had wrapped around his arm and trapped it to his chest. He struggled with it as its dry lips ran up and down his visor, broken teeth chomping in his face. It dragged its tongue against his visor, leaving an ashy streak, all while the second head rolled loosely on its neck carelessly and unconcerned.

Grunting, Tommy collapsed into the wall. He balled his free hand into a fist and punched the side of the chomping head. It smashed through like a rotten Halloween pumpkin, and Tommy grabbed ahold of the brittle skull inside. Its eyes rolled around as Tommy gripped the rotten pieces of the brain and peeled it off. The parasitic strands reached up and wrapped around his finger, pulling it farther inside the skull. The second head leaned forward and chewed uselessly on Tommy's elbow.

Fighting for life, he ground his teeth and roared as he pried it off. The arm around his waist snapped off, and Tommy could see everything was held together by the impossibly strong parasitic wisps. He turned and slammed the creature against the wall, pushing hard with his trapped arm. He then jerked backward and thrust his free arm down through the stretched wisps. They snapped back like a tight curtain, and the creature fell off him.

But the next was already on top of him.

He'd been too busy to even hear it come up from behind. It wrapped its hands around his chin and yanked against his head, threatening to pull his magnet-locked helmet completely off.

Red danger signals flashed inside his helmet, alerting him to a threat from behind.

"No shit!" he screamed at the signals.

Tommy let the broken creature fall into the water and then put his foot up onto the wall, pushing back hard. He and the once-man behind him stumbled back and splashed into the water. He came up just as the eye stalk broke the water's surface. A huge, fat eye blinked madly. With all the strength in his arm, Tommy punched the creature in the eye, bursting the lid and letting dark jelly leak out. The creature rose from the water, but Tommy had already gotten to his knees and pulled his rifle from his shoulder. He let off a burst at point-blank range until there was a fist-sized hole in its chest.

Huffing, he got to his feet and stumbled backward. When neither of the creatures came after him, he turned around and sprinted as quickly as he could.

He took small gasps of air as he got further away from the room, still half worried they might come crawling after him. He stood in the hallway that led to the cafeteria, breathing hard. Up ahead, he could see a bright, flickering light shining out into the hall.

That must be the room with the security monitors.

He was surprised how much he remembered about the layout of the station. The lights were weak, but the power was working.

Take a moment. Catch your breath.

He found a new hallway door and stepped up to the entrance panel. The scanner light came on, and he angled it down to his badge.

"Access," he said.

CALL OF THE VOID

It scanned, and a red light on the door turned green. *"Access granted,"* the doors responded and opened.

The room was dark, but he stepped in, rifle raised with the light passing over the equipment. The door closed behind him.

When he saw it was empty, he said, "Lights. Power on."

The lights flickered and turned on. Several monitors came to life as code blinked across them.

He looked around the room once more. When he was certain he was alone, he let his rifle drop loosely on his shoulder to hang on its strap. And feeling suddenly claustrophobic, he reached up and pressed the release buttons on his helmet.

A motor inside his CAG whined, and the magnets came loose. His helmet popped up, and he took it off.

He breathed hard and turned it around. He could see the ashy smears still coating his lens. He spotted an old jacket and used the material to wipe it clean, but it only streaked across the visor, likely making it all the worse to see.

"Fuck," he hissed and worked harder, but the filth was thick. In a rage, he reared up, ready to throw his helmet at a wall, but something else caught his eye.

The vid-screen was showing a room he hadn't yet been in. There were many creatures, each unique in its design, but one stood out amongst them all.

"The hell is that. . ." The color drained from his face as he studied the screen.

It could be fifteen or twenty feet tall, possibly more, but it seemed bent because of how small the room was. Wild, thick tentacles moved and waved around it in surreal motions.

The other creatures seemed humbly bowed before it, and they were dragging up a person. Tommy could clearly see the person was in a CAG.

The person was weakly fighting against them. It was hard to see who it—

No. . .

As she turned her face, Tommy realized who it was. He'd been with her just a short time ago.

Tanaka.

The thought squeezed the breath from his chest.

I'm too late.

The other creatures stayed bowed in apparent submission. Offering Tanaka as some sacrifice to a greater beast.

The larger creature reached out for her, picking her up, its mouth opening wide—

Tommy looked away, thankful that there was no sound. He couldn't watch what came next, not to Tanaka.

When he looked back, she was lying on the floor, unmoving.

Focus. Tanaka is dead but there might be others.

Tommy took a seat at the desk and clicked over the cameras. He tried to view the cafeteria, but the camera came up dead. Possibly damaged or simply malfunctioning—he didn't know and didn't have time to find out. He clicked through the other cameras to find the best route to the cafeteria and settled on how to get there. There didn't appear to be anything between him and a direct route to there.

He pressed the button for his comms and called in vain, "Commander Tealson, do you copy?" He waited a few moments. "Does anyone copy?"

There was no response.

Cursing under his breath, he looked at his helmet once more and decided the smear was still passable. He put it back on his head, and it sank into place, sealing with a hissing sound.

"Here we go."

Tommy headed back into the hallway and made his way out, trudging for a few quiet minutes before he heard the sounds of creatures.

He froze in place, mentally making plans of running back to the safety of the monitor room, but then he realized the sounds weren't coming closer.

They were already in the cafeteria.

He moved closer—his rifle raised—and saw what was happening.

A mob of flesh and hunger was collected at a door in the far corner. They were screaming and banging against the wall, trying to get inside. He wasn't sure what he was going to do, but he had to try to help somehow.

Oh God, there are so many of them.

Tommy leaned back and tried his comms again, whispering this time: "This is Reeves. Does anyone copy?"

Finally he heard a response, though the transmission was still choppy. "—*eeves... copy... advise... ack. I re—*"

Tommy tapped his helmet furiously, trying in vain to improve the transmission quality.

Shit, shit, SHIT!

"—*et back... plosion.*"

Tommy heard the door crash in and watched as the horde of creatures went through to claim their prize.

He didn't think—he couldn't. If he did, he'd only lean back and let it all happen. Instead, he sprinted mindlessly forward, hoping to catch some of the things by surprise with an attack from behind. With his XTU rifle raised high, he prayed he didn't catch a stray bullet as Tealson's team fired on the creatures from the kitchen. But then he heard a hissing sound.

Plosion...

Pure instinct grabbed Tommy, and he jumped into a dining booth, using the back to shield himself from the debris of the blast.

There was a flash of light and a near-deafening sound. Tealson's broken transmission had been warning him to stay back, that they were going to cause an explosion—he knew that now. The booth rocked hard, and his head shook inside his helmet, dazing him. He was nearly thrown into the air.

He breathed hard as the whole world went silent...

Tealson's plan had worked.

...but the silence lasted only a moment.

The screams started. Terrible sounds came from somewhere—or was it from everywhere at once? He blinked hard, trying to focus his vision, and the screaming grew in intensity.

Tommy held his head in both hands, waiting for it to stop spinning. He opened his eyes when he realized the screaming still hadn't stopped, and then he saw why. Gore had painted the entire room, and he had wet pieces of something—hopefully not some*one*—on his arm.

The water from the floor had been thrown up in the air from the explosion. But now it was long, frozen shards that showed the exact direction the water had been going when the force threw it.

The creatures were still there. Almost all of them dead. A few quivered on the floor, frozen in place. One was impaled by an icy javelin, and it meekly worked its hands against the ice trying to get free.

Another had its head frozen entirely to the floor, and its legs kept pushing at the ground, trying to get out. There were still more, but the fight had been taken out of them. They were dazed and defeated.

Explosion must have blown a cryo tank.

Tommy leaned up, feeling the solidity of the uneven ice below his feet. He stepped down carefully, still holding onto the booth for support. Some of the surviving creatures turned to look at him with dull eyes. They reached at him with broken fingers, and snapped with their loose, ragged jaws. He'd thought just moments ago they were finally defeated.

No. They're still hungry.

They still moaned and screamed as he carefully stepped past them. He shouted toward the back room. "Commander! Is everyone okay?"

Several of the creatures were in the doorway. They'd taken the brunt of the explosion and all appeared to be dead. Simply corpses frozen to the ground.

"That you, Reeves?" Tealson yelled back, but his voice was pained. "We're all fine, but some of us are injured."

"Let's just get the hell out of here!" Elliot yelled.

Tommy raised his rifle and carefully trained it on a creature that looked like it would pop to life at any moment.

"We get them all out there?" Tealson called over.

Tommy looked across the cafeteria floor. Nothing appeared to be able to attack them.

"They're not all dead, but I think they're all incapacitated." Tommy saw one tentacle squirm and stretch in his direction, but it was frozen to the floor. "Sooner we get out of here, the better."

"Fuck yeah," DalBon called over to him, and Tommy could see him through the doorway. "It's going to be a bitch digging through this shit."

Tommy nodded. "Can you climb over it?"

"Negative," Tealson said. "My damn foot is frozen to the ground." He groaned. "Elliot and Becks are hurt too. But I think we'll be okay, for the most part."

"Yeah, it got my knee," Becks yelled back.

One of the frozen corpses in the doorway had an eye open. Tommy watched as it slowly shifted to look at him.

"Shit," Tommy hissed, pointing his rifle at it. "We better get a move on."

"Well, don't wait too long, princess," DalBon said, smirking between the gaps. "Start chiseling through these assholes."

With an audible sigh, Tommy turned his rifle over and used the butt to slam against a frozen creature. An arm cracked off from its frozen torso and blood leaked.

"Fucking ridiculous," Tommy hissed under his breath as he raised his rifle again.

10

Braun stepped into the office as the others barricaded the door. It was, of course, an unnecessary exercise, but he didn't concern himself with what made those of lesser minds feel more secure and less threatened.

Strange. . . they feel that if a creature were capable of getting through a reinforced steel door, that it could then be slowed down by oddly-arranged furniture.

They were in the sector chief's cabin. A multi-roomed private quarters. Braun had never seen the inside before, but noted, with mild irritation, it was triple the size of his own cabin.

Yet, the man never produced a damn thing of value beyond the attempt at a balanced budget.

The thought made him snort. They'd failed even at that. An ever-ballooning budget deficit coupled with terrible mismanagement and poor insight led the Felicity base to near uselessness. It had been that way when his team had arrived years ago, working on a government black budget and on operations too sensitive for the prying eyes of Earth.

It was at that point Felicity finally started to produce something useful.

We heard a knock.

The vivid memory came with startling speed, making him bump into a table. He straightened as the memory replayed in his mind. He analyzed it and his feelings. Was this something of remorse? Regret?

Surely not. He just wasn't feeling well under the circumstances.

He glanced back at the people with him. Two of them were hugging. They were possibly a married couple. It struck him as somewhat odd that he hadn't noticed before.

You've been occupied. Trying to work through a particularly difficult puzzle. It is understandable.

It was true. He hadn't meant for any of this to happen. That was clear to everyone. He would have liked nothing more than to have continued with his work. Of course, if he had the chance to redo things, he would've been more cautious. Under the circumstances, however, he could admit he was the catalyst for the situation. But to find blame for something no one could have perceived? Well, that was something he would not do.

You did as any would. There is nothing to apologize for.

"Braun?" A man stuck his head out of a connecting room and motioned for him to enter. "Come here." The man was bald with a neatly trimmed, brown beard and small eyebrows, which Braun thought made the rest of his face look particularly fat.

Braun walked into the small office, leaving the others to cry within the living room. "What?" he said, not caring to hide the tiredness in his voice.

The man had already taken the sector chief's seat behind a large mahogany desk that must have cost a small fortune to haul to Mars. Accolades for the dead man lined the wall, and a computer monitor sat on the desk. The room was completely untouched by everything that had happened. The sealed door had even kept even the water out until Braun and the others entered.

"Look what I found." The bald man hauled up a bottle of whiskey from a desk drawer and set it down. "And look here. Apparently he kept company in his office." He came up with two small glasses and placed them on the desk. He took the top of the bottle off and poured a small bit into each glass. When he was done, he motioned for Braun to sit and then picked up his glass, taking a drink.

Braun was not a drinker. He stood, unmoving, and watched the man, waiting for him to get to the point.

The man snorted and shook his head. "Just sit down, Braun. We need to talk."

Braun took in a deep breath of stale air and exhaled loudly before sitting down. "I hope this is important. And quick."

The bald man nodded, and light gleamed off his head. "You're a smart man, Braun. We all know that. Without you, we would not have gotten from the cryo room to here." The man lifted his shoulders in an earnest gesture. "I know that. You make good, calculated decisions. It's clear to everyone."

"Agreed," Braun said somewhat sarcastically.

The man pointed at Braun. "Here's the thing, though." He stopped to down the rest of his drink and then poured himself another. "We're all smart people here, and I think we need to slow down, catch our breath, and analyze the situation."

Braun watched him carefully. "What is your name?"

"Rodney. In charge of project Crystal Care and—"

"I know of project Crystal Care. I read your reports. You are testing the strength of drills on Mars' core. Possible mining operations."

Smartly, Rodney bowed his head.

"It was eight months late and three times over budget."

Rodney barked a laugh and took a drink. "I didn't know what you were working on. No one did. You had a nice, little black-budget defense order, and you were tucked away in your little corner of our station. And while I was eight months late and *four* times over budget, I didn't open a goddamn gate and let some aliens run their asses in here, now did I?"

Braun took the point. "They're not aliens. Not in the way you mean them anyway."

"That's fine." Rodney swirled his drink in his hand. "*Semantics*. Here's my idea, though. When I look in that room over there," he pointed over Braun's shoulder, "I see Michael Gardenier, a researcher in animal cell growth. I see Lesliann Raper, neurophysicist and psychologist. I see—"

"There's also a botanist. What's your point?"

"Point *is*, we're not a bunch of fools. I think we all need to have a *seat*." He emphasized the word and motioned for Braun to sit once more. "Catch our breath, and talk over what we're dealing with here."

Braun was tired and cold. Running through flooded hallways with a barely functioning heat system while breathing air that tasted like it had been pumped from a tomb could do that to a person—part mechanical or otherwise.

"Okay." Braun took the seat. Rodney gestured to the drink, but Braun shook his head.

It was clear to Braun that Rodney saw this as a project, one he could try to manage. He called in both Michael and Lesliann, and the two had a seat. They'd each gotten a drink and tried to calm their nerves. The others were going through the rooms, searching for anything useful.

"Here's what I think," Michael said, steepling his hands in front of him. "We really need to put a name to what it is we're seeing."

Lesliann took a long sip and set her cup down. She bobbed her head and wiped a strand of hair behind her ear. "I agree. If we classify them, we can have a better idea of what we're dealing with."

Braun frowned. Had this only just now occurred to them?

"From what I gather," Rodney said as he leaned back in his chair, looking as if he was in a business appointment rather than sitting behind a dead man's desk in a failing space station, "we've seen at least two classifications. One posthuman. The other not."

Lesliann shook her head. "Posthuman suggests a superior quality. These seem. . ." She struggled for a word. "*Ridden*."

"*Ridden*," Braun said the word in a way that implied it was stupid.

"What are they, Braun?" Michael asked. "They are people who change after coming into contact with the *other* beings."

"It's clear to me that they're parasites," Braun said. "Any penetration of the skin risks infection."

Rodney's eyes narrowed as he listened carefully. "And how have you come to that conclusion?"

"I've seen the *ridden* moving without heads. I suspected as such. I confirmed it when Dr. Conners was pushed into the airlock. I saw it moving beneath his skin."

They'd all been complacent with pushing their colleague into the airlock. None had argued as Braun tapped the commands and dropped him onto Mars.

Still, it brought a moment of quiet to the discussion.

"So it's clear, then." Rodney swirled his glass. "Being wounded by the others can produce a *ridden* quality."

"Yeah, so don't let them touch you," Lesliann said sarcastically, staring into her glass.

"And the *others*?" Michael asked. "You opened a gate and brought them here? They're from another system than ours? Foreign invaders? *Aliens*?"

"No," Braun said and then took a moment to think better of it. "Perhaps. It remains uncertain. What is clear is that *alien* implies a certain *extraterrestrial* quality. These are extra*dimensional*. They could potentially even be *of Earth*, but not Earth as we would know it."

"Fascinating." Rodney took another taste. "Would be even more so if they weren't trying to eat us."

"Hmm." Lesliann rubbed her chin. "What makes you certain that you reached a new reality?"

While the discussion was not as irritating as Braun had expected, and the moment to catch his breath was appreciated, he did find such useless questions hard to answer with a respectful tone. "Care to elaborate your reasoning for the question?"

"What I mean is, have you not considered that you punched a hole straight into *Hell*?" she asked.

"Don't be ridiculous," Braun said.

"How is that ridiculous?" Michael asked. "What is Hell if not another dimension parallel to our own?"

"Somehow I doubt Lucifer is an eyeless creature that spreads parasites with bites."

"Really? Because that sounds exactly like Hell to me," Michael said.

Rodney held up a hand. "Let's put their origins to bed for the moment. Consider their attributes. The others. The *elites*." They all knew what he was talking about.

The ones that came through the gates.

"Elites." Braun rubbed his chin. "Yes, I suppose that is a good way to refer to them. They were native to whatever reality they came through. They are not—nor have they ever been—human."

"They have no single design," Michael said. "No general bone structure or appendages."

"Yes, but they do have some similar qualities." Lesliann held up one finger. "A pink to pale-white color of skin." Another finger. "No eyes." A third finger. "Large mouths that seem to peel like fruit. And teeth. Lots of teeth."

They do not breathe," Braun said. "They do not see. They do not hear. And likely, they do not smell."

"How can they tell where we're at, then?" Rodney asked.

"My leading consideration is that their skin is sensitive to vibration. They feel through the ground. It's possible that they may *hear* in the sense that vibrations of sounds hit their flesh."

"So, when they are nearby, we do not move at all?" Michael asked, holding his hands up as if they'd all reached a particularly useful conclusion. "I mean, it's particularly hard not to make noise while sloshing through standing water."

Braun cut in, "I suspect the sensitivity is different between creatures. Some seem particularly more attentive than others. Perhaps our breathing would be enough to alert some. Possibly even the beat of a heart would be enough for others. It's hard to say."

"Let's hope that's not the case, as I'd like to have my heart remain beating," Rodney said.

Braun felt the beginnings of a smile curl on his lips.

"Have you named them?" Rodney asked.

"Have I named *what*?" Braun asked.

"The creatures. You were the first to make contact. Have you named them?"

"Mark Rufus did." It was strange. Braun hadn't thought of it in some time. "He called the first one Cronus. Leader of the Titans in Greek mythology. That certainly couldn't apply to them as a whole though."

"Cronux, then," Michael said. "Close enough, and a name as good as any."

Braun considered it. He didn't have a better suggestion.

Rodney downed the last of his drink. "Okay, then. What is our next course of action, Braun?"

THERE WAS A SECURITY ROOM NEARBY. If Braun was not mistaken, it had an internal comms system that should be able to make contact with other rooms through wiring rather than radio, as well as an ability to open and unlock other doors.

It wasn't far from the sector chief's cabin, but the area was more dangerous than Braun would have liked. He agreed to travel alone.

They opened the doors, and more water rushed in while Braun stepped out. The doors closed behind him, and Braun was alone. He sloshed through the water, stopping at times to listen for anything nearby. Little sounds seemed to dance off walls occasionally, mixing with the whirring in his head and his own internal monologue.

Simple. Paranoia.

Still, nothing moved, so he made his way down the corridor and to the security room. He got to the keypad and clicked a few buttons. The panel on the door slid open, and a facial-recognition device scanned his face.

The light blinked red.

"Irritating." He mumbled. He didn't have access. He had, of course, prepared for this and had taken the sector chief's extra badge from his desk drawer. He scanned the badge.

The light blinked red.

"Hmm." Braun considered.

Something clicked further away, like a wet tongue off the roof of a mouth. Braun slowly turned to glance in that direction. The water was shifting around, but he couldn't see because of the bend in the hallway.

Something was coming.

Unfortunate.

He looked back to the keypad. The badge should have worked.

Possibly, it was old and out of date and not the spare Braun had assumed it was.

The barcode was wet, Braun wiped it off with his finger. He scanned it again.

The light blinked red.

"*Scheisse,*" Braun hissed. He looked down the corridor once more in enough time to see a long, bony and fleshy leg extend into view.

Hurry.

The equipment was old. Faulty. Sensitive. He looked at the badge once more and grabbed the corner of his jacket, using it to wipe away the water.

That was when he heard the splashing.

Rapid breath, hungry for meat. Water sloshing.

It was coming quickly.

Braun held the badge up, and the light turned green.

"Access," Braun spat hastily.

"Access granted." The door opened. The water instantly flooded into the otherwise dry room, and he pressed the lock. It closed just as he saw a pinkish, long-fingered hand reach into view.

Fate plays its jokes once more.

Braun exhaled. His nerves were crawling up his spine. The room was particularly cold, and the lighting was bad. "Lights. Full," he commanded, and an extra set of lights blinked pathetically to life.

Braun stopped. He was not alone.

A man was sitting in a desk chair and staring out the window to Mars. There was a large hole out the top of his head and a pistol sitting on his chest, his finger still gripping the trigger.

The man looked emaciated. Likely he'd been able to get into the room, but was stuck here for some time before hearing the call of the void, enticing him to just end it all.

Braun looked out the window. As far as views to end your life to, Braun supposed it could have been better.

The red, lifeless surface of Mars was all there was to gaze at.

Desolate. Desperate.

I wonder how tired he got of looking out that window while he sat here growing hungry.

The creature was still scratching at the door, hoping to open it up and dig out the fresh meat inside. Braun glanced back to the door, thankful for its security, but after a moment's consideration, he looked at the dead man.

He'd likely been in a similar situation.

Braun could only speculate how long the creature would wait, but if the starved dead man was any indication...

Inconvenient.

He flipped on switches and waited for systems to undergo their reboot. He rolled the chair with the dead man to a corner, and then tilted it up, letting the man flop to the floor. Glancing around, he found a worker's glove, which he used to brush off the cold, dried pieces of brain from the top of the chair. He wheeled the chair back to the desk and sat down in front of the monitor.

He turned on the vid-screen and saw cameras all over the base come to life. Some were damaged, others were dead completely, but most were clear.

There was Leonard on one screen. He was the man that foolishly opposed Braun and didn't follow him. The creatures, which Lesliann had dubbed *ridden,* splayed out on the floor. They were eating him. Leonard was struggling and screaming. Thankfully, there was no audio. It was particularly odd, though, that Leonard still lived and had not changed.

Either they chose not to embed a parasite into him, or not everyone turns. Curious.

He watched for a few moments longer before he clicked to the next camera.

The video for the gate room brought a smile to his lips. They'd shorted out one of the conduits, and it looked to be only partially functioning, blinking in and out.

Something else staggered into view.

A frighteningly large creature, so big it would certainly have trouble making it through most doorways. It was large and multi-legged with thick tentacles stretching out and undulating as it moved.

Braun watched closely, noting how the smaller ones, large in their own right, deferred and bowed before it.

Clearly, it was something special.

He looked away—leaving it for another time—and saw people in the cafeteria. They looked to have barely survived a recent encounter.

Excellent.

Braun reached for the comms system command but hesitated. It was blinking red.

Malfunction. Scheisse.

He typed in new commands and clicked to the camera in the docking bay area. He took command of it and swiveled to look around. He could see his rescuers' ship, but there was no way to hail it directly, not without a radio connection. He'd already attempted that some time ago. All there was left was the direct, wired, room-to-room communications.

But if there was no one in the room, they would not see his awaiting call.

Grunting now, the thing at the door smashed into it again. He clicked the button for communications, and through his camera saw the light in the comms station inside the docking bay blink green, indicating an incoming call.

Now all he had to do... was wait.

LACEY MOLLER PACED INSIDE the *Perihelion's* bridge, feeling particularly useless as a communications specialist. There was just no boosting the signal to reach anyone. She'd tried every little trick she'd ever learned, but nothing worked.

Nothing.

But that didn't mean she was going to stop trying.

She'd tried killing code and diverting energy resources. It failed. She tried boosting power from non-critical equipment. It also failed.

As did the next thing and the next after that and the next after that. . . Whatever was interfering with the signal, it was something she'd never come across before. All that seemed to work was getting some distance from Mars, and everything would start working again. Other than diverting *all* power to boost the signal, and possibly crippling the ship, she was out of ideas.

"It's those goddamn Russians. You know it is," Bennie said, pointing at Stalls. "Who else would be out here, mucking shit up like this? Those bastards are always—"

"Bennie, if you keep saying that shit," Stalls cut in, "I'm going to pull out my sidearm and shoot you in the head." She seemed to think for a moment and added, "Or, at the very least, a good pistol-whipping."

That was new. Flight staff weren't cleared for weapons for fear of an accidental firing, but Tealson had given Stalls the okay to retrieve her weapon from a lockbox.

Not having one made Moller feel naked.

She let out a sigh, as she continued to think, but self doubt was pulling her under.

You're useless. Tanaka strapped on a CAG, but you're just here. A waste of space and oxygen.

Moller didn't want to go out. Who the hell would? But she hated feeling like she wasn't carrying her weight.

Bennie held up his hands. "All right, all right! Don't have to tell me twice." He snatched a plain, metal cup off the dashboard and took a drink. He was silent for all of three seconds before he said, "Just sayin', you know it was them."

"At the moment, I don't give a *fuck* who it was. I just want to get out of here." Stalls turned to look out the cockpit window.

All that was out there was the big, empty cargo room. Moller should know, as she'd spent enough time looking out there herself.

"What the hell do you think is going on out there, Bennie?" Stalls asked. "I mean, for real. And I don't want to hear about the Russians."

Sighing, Bennie said, "Well, if it ain't the Russians, it's aliens, just like Tealson said. Not where my money's at, but. . ." he trailed off. They both sat quietly before Bennie looked over at Moller. "How about you, kid? What do you think about all this?"

Moller smiled politely but didn't look at him. "I don't know what to think."

"But you're glad you've got a view, right?" Bennie joked and waved toward the window and the empty cargo hold. They'd been looking at it for hours now.

She looked out, hoping against hope to see the door open and the rest of her crew returning. Instead, she saw the same empty room, barren walls and—

There was a blinking green light on a power unit.

"What's that?" she pointed.

Bennie walked closer to the window, looking around. "What's what?"

"Down there by the door. See? It's blinking."

Squinting, Bennie shook his head. "No idea."

Stalls came up alongside him and looked. "*Shit,*" she whispered. "That's a room-to-room comms system."

"A what?" Moller asked, confused.

"Internal comms. All wiring. From the goddamn eighties." Stalls straightened up. "Someone is calling us."

"Hot damn." Bennie leaned up and adjusted his pants. "How about you both sit here and I'll—"

"I'll go," Moller interjected. She took a hair tie out of her pocket and pulled her hair back.

"Well, wait a second here." Bennie held up his hand. "No need for you to—"

"It's fine. I want to go. I hate feeling useless."

"How about—" Bennie started.

"Son of a bitch, Bennie," Stalls scoffed. "She's not a kid, let her go." She eyed Moller. "You'll need to get an all-atmosphere suit on before you go, and we better hurry." She looked at Bennie. "Keep the cockpit warm, will you?"

Holding his hands up in disbelief, Bennie watched as they left.

Moller and Stalls hurried down to the hold. Moller had already begun to strip down. She was down to just her shirt and underwear, leaving a trail with her boots, jacket, and pants when she got to the hold.

Stalls helped her get into the suit. "They said the air is breathable." Stalls planted her helmet on and let it magnetically seal. "But I wouldn't trust my life to it." She adjusted the last part, closing off the suit. "Don't do anything stupid. You're not in CAG."

Moller nodded.

"Here." Stalls stripped her pistol out of her holster, chambered a round, and handed it to Moller. "Better safe than sorry, right?"

"Thank you."

It wasn't long after that the ship was opening and she stepped off alone.

The whole atmosphere changed when she was no longer in a nice, metal cocoon.

As she moved toward the comms, she felt like the shadows against the wall were going to peel off and kill her.

She closed in on the comms station, and now she remembered it from her textbooks. They were relics that were mostly nonfunctional on Earth, but were apparently still in use here.

The green light kept blinking, inviting her in, whispering in a soothing voice that *everything is okay. Everything will be fine. Just push the little button.*

She reached her gloved hand out and pressed it.

"Hello?" she said.

A harsh and distinct voice answered, *"This is Will Braun. With whom am I speaking?"*

A GIRL HAD ANSWERED. Through the camera, she looked to be a thin and frail thing. But as Braun had impatiently waited for someone to answer the comm, he had clicked to a camera that was near his location and punched in commands, taking direct control of it and using the arrow keys to make it swivel.

It had turned, whining surely, and focused on his door.

The creature was there. Still waiting.

And it would be for far too long. It would wait for hours or possibly days, and at that time, the men in the cafeteria may have already died or left.

Braun had brought up the door operating system, a system built for emergencies. Tapping away at the keys, he began to set his course and command certain doors to unlock and open, while closing others. He hoped to give the creatures an easier path to the other side of the base and away from him.

When the girl answered, Braun began thinking. He had a new problem.

How was he going to get out of here?

"This is Officer Lacey Moller of Orbital Corps," she said. "We've been looking for you. How many people are there with you?"

Braun considered. The creature was still in front of his door. Still waiting.

It needed a distraction.

He pressed the command to force open the sector chief's cabin, where Rodney and the others still were.

The sound of the opening door drew the creature's attention.

"Only me," Braun said.

11

ALICE FELT a moment of relief as they neared the med lab. The lights were fully functional along with the security systems. She got to the door lock and aimed the scanner at her badge. A small light lit up green.

"Access," she said.

The door responded, *"Access granted,"* and slid open.

"Dammit," Bartlet groaned as they walked in. "That *thing* is still alive."

The creature on the ground—a woman formerly known as Lyndsay Waters—still had its hand poked out from beneath the furniture they'd thrown on top of it. Its wretched hand was still clawing at the ground as Bartlet walked over and crushed it with the heel of his boot, cracking the small bones with a sickening crunch.

"Is that necessary?" Alice hissed, helping carry Smith. It wasn't particularly hard to lug him around with the added strength of the CAG.

"Sure was." Bartlet sneered as he looked up. "I hate this place. I hate this whole *goddamn* place."

"Not exactly my favorite either," Smith mumbled as they got him onto a medical table.

"Bartlet, be useful and go lock that door," Alice said, doing little to hide the disdain in her voice.

"Roger that," he said sarcastically as he went to the door and hit the large, red *lock* key.

Alice turned to Smith. "We're going to have to get your CAG off."

"Can I breathe without it?" Smith was pale and sweating, his face looking like rubber.

She nodded. "You can. Air is breathable. Just going to taste like shit."

"I can deal with it. I'm feeling claustrophobic anyway. Get this damn thing off me." Smith reached up and undid the clasps on his helmet. Air burst free as it decompressed, and he dropped it to the floor with a hollow thud. He used the back of his wrist to wipe sweat off his face. "You were right," he said as he took a deep breath and made a face. "It's certainly *breathable*, but smells like a dead cat's ass."

"I don't like it in here," Bartlet whispered as he looked out the door's windows. "We're cornered. No exit. Nowhere to go if they grind us to the wall..."

"The door is locked, Bartlet. This is one of the most secure rooms in the whole facility. Take it easy, and just keep an eye out." She undid the clasps around Smith's arm. They popped off with loud clicks. She pulled the glove off. Black veins had worked down toward his fingers and—

Something was moving beneath the skin.

She imagined a sheet pulled tight, and someone beneath it dragging their finger down it. It pushed up against the skin and squirmed before fading.

It was crawling.

Oh my God...

Smith hadn't seen it, but he could surely feel it. He only stared at the ceiling, wincing as Alice moved his arm around. She'd never seen anything like it, and the very sight made her stomach crawl.

Keep it together.

She undid the clasps around his arm and pulled the whole sleeve down. Smith groaned and ground his teeth, as she took it off and dumped it on the floor.

"*It burns,*" he whispered.

Was it nerve damage? Muscle tearing? She didn't know.

His entire arm was riddled with black scars, but there was a solid lump just beneath the skin of his bicep.

Her eyes went wide. "I see it, Smith. Just hang with me."

"I've got shit for options here, lady," he said and gritted his teeth.

Alice hurried toward the back of the med lab, past Lyndsay, and to the equipment locker.

Silently, she prayed it would have the tools she needed.

The room was well-lit, but a single light in the back kept blinking, seemingly with the same rhythm as the beat of Alice's heart.

Everything here on Mars seemed to move and react with strange purpose. As if the entire facility was a living beast speaking in a language no one understood.

You're going to die here, it said. *Everyone is going to die here.*

Ignoring the clawing dread, she rifled through the locker and found the kit and tools she needed. Desperate to scratch an itch on her forehead that was impossible to get, she only closed her eyes and swallowed.

Get your shit together.

The facility's power had been off for too long, so she needed to disinfect her equipment. She took her tools and kit over to a sterilizer and turned it on. It was an old model that looked like an oversized microwave but should be adequate as long as it powered up.

She punched numbers into the keypad, and it buzzed to life, flashing a blue light down onto the tools for half a minute before turning off.

Flexing her CAG gloves in front of her, she tested their feel. She should be able to sanitize them too and perform delicate medical work, but they didn't feel right. After a moment's consideration, she popped their clasps and pulled the gloves off, setting them aside. She tugged on blue rubber gloves instead.

She got the utensils out of the sterilizer and took them down by

Smith, placing the tray within reach.

This wasn't a sterile room by any stretch of the imagination, but this was the best she could do for him.

"I'm going to have to put you under, Smith," she said as she arranged the tools on a tray.

"Fuck that idea. You're not knocking me out. Just dope me." Smith gave a humorless laugh and grinned, showing his bad teeth.

"This is going to hurt. It's going to hurt a *lot*."

"I don't care. I'm staying awake."

"Okay, just lay back then." She reached down for the straps on either side and leashed them through, drawing them tight. She rolled over a second, smaller table and strapped his arm to it.

The black lines were crawling higher, and whatever was beneath his skin was still squirming.

A tear rolled down Smith's face. "I can feel the little shit moving inside me. It's climbing up my damn arm."

"I'm going to get it out of you," Alice said with as much confidence as she could muster.

As if the thing heard them, it squirmed more, leaving a loose pocket of skin as it went deeper into his arm. A thumb-sized parasite, digging its way around inside his bicep.

In a perfect world, she would have a clean facility, several assistants, and the best medical equipment.

But in a perfect world, there wouldn't be a parasite crawling under this guy's skin. You just have to make do.

Glancing back, she saw Bartlet was still staring out the window. Blind and deaf to what was happening to them.

Practically useless.

She cursed him silently as she grabbed the utensils. She plunged a syringe into a vial and drew in its contents, feeding it into Smith's arm to numb him.

"Come here," she said to Bartlet. "I need you to work the suction."

With a grunt, Bartlet came over. He didn't complain, but clearly he didn't want to be here.

Like anyone does.

"Suction the blood when it starts to pool," Alice said, handing him the tool.

"Fine," Bartlet responded.

"Don't fuck it up, man. That's the arm I beat off with." Smith braved a grin, and Bartlet croaked out a laugh.

"You're going to feel a pinch," Alice said as she grabbed the scalpel from the tray. "Just don't look."

Smith said nothing as she squeezed the lump between two fingers and slid the scalpel over the lifted skin. He only squeezed his eyes shut and turned away.

The scalpel split the skin open just as cleanly as if his arm had a zipper. Blood leaked, but Bartlet took care of it.

There.

A wet, purple nub was squirming around. It didn't like being exposed. It looked like a raw piece of intestine with small, blue veins threading through it.

Squeezing her fingers on either side of it, Alice grabbed her forceps and worked them around the creature's sides. She pulled, but the parasite writhed and twisted, making the forceps slide off.

Shit.

Smith groaned. Clearly, he could still feel it moving around.

Alice slid the forceps around it again and pinched tighter. The parasite's flesh quaked like jelly, clearly in pain. She squeezed the forceps and pulled. Smith groaned as the fat little purple thing slowly emerged from his arm. One of the parasite's thin wisps curled out like fishing wire. It spiraled around in a circle as it slid out of Smith's arm and then whipped around.

"*Dammit,*" Alice whispered as it lightly smacked against her finger and tried to loop around it.

She jerked back, and Bartlet shouted as he knocked a tray on accident, scattering everything to the floor.

"Wha—what's it doing?" Smith asked, his voice quivering.

Neither of them answered. Alice braved forward and stuck her finger out. The wisp wrapped around it, and she pulled it taut.

Little shit.

She grabbed a scalpel and sliced it through the wisp. It fell to the floor like useless string.

"Nasty fucker!" Bartlet slammed his heel down and dragged his boot over it, leaving a clear liquid smeared on the floor with the twitching wisp.

The parasite thrashed and squirmed, digging into Smith's arm.

"Fuck!" Smith shouted, the veins in his neck popping. "Oh God, it hurts! *It hurts!*"

Alice pinched her fingers around the outside of the flesh and squeezed. If she couldn't pull it out, she was going to cut it out. She dragged the scalpel across the parasite's back and black-blue blood squirted out, hitting Bartlet's visor.

"Goddammit!" Bartlet stomped back again and threw the suction equipment against the wall. "I've had *enough* of this bullshit! I'm fucking *done!*"

Alice ignored him as she struggled with the parasite. Amidst Smith's screams, it dug down between his muscle strands, somehow sliding between the muscle fibers and going deeper.

The pain must have been too great, as Smith flopped down, silent as a dead fish.

With all the strength she had, Alice squeezed the arm, trying to pop the parasite up so she could dig it out with the scalpel, but it was a fruitless endeavor.

It wasn't coming out. It was staying in Smith's arm, and it was going to turn him.

His veins had already darkened another shade as it reached up toward his shoulder and soon to his neck.

The wisps were heading to his brain.

Smith was a dead man.

No, he's not.

Alice's guts twisted as she turned to look at Bartlet, her voice firm and cutting through any disagreements. "Bartlet."

He looked up, wiping the dark, sticky blood off his visor with his wrist.

"Get the saw."

12

TEALSON'S PLAN HAD WORKED. The blast had taken out most of the creatures.

But they weren't dead.

"Some of these things are still alive," Parker said. "They're still moving. You broke 'em down to little pieces, and they're still. . ." He narrowed his gaze, leaning down to look at one still frozen in ice, though snapped in half. One of its hands was free, and its fingers still moved. ". . . still alive."

"Go ahead and take a piss on them for all I care," Elliot huffed.

When the kitchen door had opened, the blast had taken most of the creatures out.

But they hadn't calculated the impact on the cryo tanks.

The blast had released their fluids, and the water froze near instantly—so fast that it even caught the water still in the air.

A shard of it had hit Elliot's helmet, so sharp and cold it left a deep groove down the side of his visor. A sharp piece of ice had hit Becks in the knee, knocking him over, but he was fine.

Parker and DalBon had managed to get off the floor and away from the water, but Tealson had had no such luck, having one foot submerged in water as it had frozen.

It had all happened in the blink of an eye, but strangely, he'd felt like he could see it coming. Unfortunately, he had been unable to move fast enough. The explosion had thrown the water a split second before it also blew the tank. The water had pooled around his foot, and he'd turned to move just as it froze, one foot in the air and the other planted.

The water had locked around him like an icy vice.

And it hurt. So cold it burned, and there was a strange, painful sensation like sandpaper rubbing over his skin.

"My damn foot is stuck." Tealson gritted his teeth and grabbed his ankle, pulling on it and groaning. "Fuck, that hurts!"

"Wait, let me see." Becks came up and looked closely, shining his helmet light around the base of Tealson's ankle. The ice had frozen hard right around his ankle. "That shit is solid. We're going to have to melt it somehow."

"And wait for something else to show up?" Tealson flashed his eyes at him. "The hell with that idea."

Becks held up his arms. "You got a better one?"

Tealson looked about the room, his helmet light shining across the kitchen utensils. It settled on a butcher knife.

He pointed at it. "Bring that to me."

A CHILL RAN down Moller's back.

She felt naked. Alone, unarmored, and exposed to anything that might crawl or lurk here.

As a child, she'd had a frequent, recurring nightmare. She would be running through a dark house with endless hallways. Something would always be chasing her, huffing and grunting for want of meat.

The dream would always end the same way, too. She'd feel the presence looming behind her, too close to escape.

It was a bloody thing as large as the hallway itself. It looked like a corpse with the meat all half-rotted and hanging in loose folds, its fingers only of blood-caked bone.

And when she'd turn around to see it...

It would grab her.

And she would wake up, drenched in sweat, her heart throbbing in her throat.

But there was no waking up here. No way to end things. And just now, with only Stalls sidearm to protect her, she imagined she could feel it right behind her, reaching up for the back of her head. And there was the persistent beat of her heart crawling up her throat.

This time she didn't look back. She kept moving forward.

Think of something else.

She demanded it of herself as she rushed through the water in the direction she knew Tealson had taken his group.

Anything.

Will Braun. She'd been the only one to talk to him, and it was important to let the others know.

Because they were going the wrong way.

"It's a pleasure to be speaking with you, Officer Moller. I was beginning to wonder if Earth had forgotten all about me," Braun had said, a hint of disdain and a clipped, German accent tinged his voice.

Moller had instantly disliked the man. There was a tone in his voice that said, *you're beneath me*, and it grated her nerves.

You don't have to like him. Just get him and get out. We're almost done.

Braun had told her that he had awoken in the cryo room, but had since made his way out. He'd seen them and was trying to meet with them by traveling through a safer portion of the facility.

"It's unfortunate that your crew took the route they did. Very unfortunate." Braun's lack of concern had been chilling.

He's a Nazi.

Or had been. She had to remind herself of that, because it was hard to rationalize why they were doing this for him, especially after hearing his voice.

He's a genius. It doesn't matter if you think he's vile—we need him.

She decided not to dwell on it.

Coming down a hallway, the lights suddenly blinked to life overhead. Air filters turned on, and the station hummed to life.

"Well, fuck yeah," someone said loudly in the distance. "Could have used a little light before."

Sounds like DalBon.

Moller hustled down the hallway to a door. There was a huge opening cut into it. She stuck her head in the gap, then climbed through.

The cafeteria was a wreck. Blood and bullet holes were everywhere. The ground was frozen solid, and there were quivering limbs there, reaching and clawing in futility.

"*Oh my God,*" she said out loud.

"Moller?" It was Tommy. "What the hell are you doing here?"

"Will Braun. . ." She took a breath. "I know where he is."

"Shit," Tommy cursed under his breath. Moller had just told him they were heading in the wrong direction.

"The good news is—" She took another breath, clearly out of air. "We know he's still alive."

"Think I might have preferred knowing he was dead so we could get the hell out of here," Tommy said.

In the doorway to the kitchen, DalBon's heavy CAG boot cracked through the wall of frozen flesh. DalBon stuck his face into view, looking excited and nervous all at once, "Hey, ya fucker. You planning to help us out here?"

"Yeah, just give me a second," Tommy said to DalBon, slinging his rifle over his shoulder. "What are you going to do, Moller?"

"I was going to head back. . ." She turned to look toward the door. "But I think I'd rather stay with you all instead of running around this place by myself." She shuddered.

"You sure? It's dangerous here, and you're not in a CAG."

"Dangerous there too. I'll keep my head down."

Tommy nodded and got to the side of the frozen creatures in the doorway. He held onto a nearby drinking fountain and kicked through the ice. Chunks of frozen bodies slid across the ground, seeping red from the new breaks, but continued to squirm and wiggle.

They broke a big enough hole that DalBon was able to slide through, his gut dragging against the ice. "Hot damn, I feel like I can breathe out here." He walked over to a corner, popping the clasps on his CAG near the crotch. Bursts of air popped and fizzed. "Better turn your head, Moller."

"What are you doing?" Tommy asked him.

"My bladder has been threatening to explode down my leg for the last hour." DalBon took himself out and aimed at a frozen creature, its jaw still snapping wildly.

"The CAGs have internal bladders, so you can piss in it." Tommy shrugged.

"That sounds pretty fucking nasty," DalBon said right before he let loose on the creature's face.

Tommy turned and snaked into the room. "You all doing okay in here?"

"Just dandy," Becks said, looking up from the floor. Tealson was sitting on his ass, frozen ankle-deep to the floor.

"Shit." Tommy looked across the room, suddenly remembering what he'd seen on the vid-screen.

What you think *you saw.*

"Where's Tanaka?"

Becks gave him a sour look and shook his head. "Didn't make it. Regal either."

Something squeezed in Tommy's chest, but he nodded, deciding not to tell them what he'd seen. Maybe they could go on thinking she'd died fast.

"Commander, Moller is here," Tommy said. "She made contact with Braun."

Elliot perked up. He and Moller had a *thing* going on the ship that was supposed to be secret, but in reality, everyone knew about it. "She's here?"

Tommy nodded to Elliot. "He's holed up not too far from here, but we were going in the wrong direction."

"Not too far?" Elliot blinked wildly as if he had sand in his eyes. "I hope she told him to go trek the rest of the way then, right?"

"Shut up," Tealson said.

Elliot grunted and shook his head, squeezing out of the room to go to Moller.

Tealson watched him leave and sighed. He looked to Tommy and shook his head. "Finally some good news, but my damn foot is stuck here."

Becks grimaced. "I tried to cut the damn thing out, but it's *solid*."

"The explosion burst a cryo tank. Froze everything quick. It's a *hard* freeze too. Won't start thawing anytime soon." Tealson huffed.

Tommy leaned down again, inspecting Tealson's foot closely. "*Shit*," he hissed. "We're going to have to try and etch out a piece of it or something."

"Negative. We don't have time to play archaeologist." Tealson said. "Parker, get over here." He waved to the larger man. "You, Becks, and Reeves get a grip below my arms. See if you can't pull me out."

Becks's eyes went wide. "That could rip your damn foot off!"

Tealson frowned. "And so could the next thing that shows up waiting for us to get out of here. Just do it."

"*Shit*," Peter spat, but did as he was told. He went behind Tealson and grabbed him.

Tommy and Parker did the same, each gripping beneath his arm.

"On three," Tommy said, "One, two, *three*."

As a group, they pulled until Tealson's body went tight like a rope. Tealson began huffing and groaning as the ice creaked, then he started screaming. "Do it! *Do it!*"

The ice cracked and snapped until, finally, he broke free. Tealson pounded a fist onto the ground, screaming as they sat him down once more. "Fuck me!" The ice broke into jagged lines under his fist. "I can't move my ankle."

"Shit!" Becks said as he looked down. "It froze through the CAG. Goddamn hand-me-downs. The boot is compromised."

The whole foot of the CAG was cracked and iced. The water had somehow gotten through the hard rubber connectors between the metal armor slates.

It's got to be on his skin too.

"Can you walk?" Tommy asked.

Tealson tried to stand but shook his head. "No, the bottom is slick, and it hurts like hell." He gritted his teeth. "Cut the damn thing off so I can move my ankle."

"*Shit*, I don't think you understand, sir. It froze through to your foot," Becks said. "You might not have a damn ankle anymore. We're going to need to carry you back to the ship."

"The hell with that. Cut the boot, and let's get a move on."

"You do it." Becks jammed the knife over to Tommy. "I ain't got the stomach for that bull shit."

Tommy blew out a puff of air. "*Shit.*" He aimed a finger at Becks. "Go find the kitchen's med kit and get a boot off one of those things outside that isn't frozen."

"You mean a boot with a goddamn foot in it? From one of those scientists-turned-monster?" Becks frowned, sickened.

"Unless you want to give him yours?" Tommy said irritably.

"Just do it," Tealson hissed.

Tommy went down on his knee, grinding his teeth together as he worked the tip of the blade between the hard rubber of the boot. "*Shit,*" he mumbled under his breath as the edge sliced through the rubber.

"Just don't bury that into my leg. I'd like to still be able to walk after this." Tealson was holding himself right below the knee.

You're never going to walk right again.

"I'll do my best." Tommy worked the knife around, getting it stuck at a point where he had to use both hands to crank it down.

Tealson leaned his head back, fighting down a scream as his fingers tightened on his leg.

Tommy worked the knife to the clasp on the boot and undid it. Air puffed as it depressurized, but it only gave a weak hiss. He pulled back a piece, but Tealson's leg remained stuck to it.

His stomach threatened to crawl out of his throat. "It froze directly to your skin. It's going to take a chunk of you with it."

"How many fucking times do I have to tell you to shut up and do it? You've got the easy part here." Tealson refused to look at it.

Tommy got his fingers beneath the grooves of the CAG. He swallowed two deep breaths and yanked it off. The sound it made as it ripped down Tealson's skin was sickening, and the blood started flowing immediately.

Tealson had fought back the scream as long as he could before it came gurgling up in a roar. He cursed and held his bleeding foot up in the air, sending Becks to vomit in the corner.

Blood ran down Tommy's fingers, and it steamed as it hit the ground.

"*Hey!*" DalBon shouted behind them. "*Something's coming!*"

Tommy turned and unslung his rifle from his shoulder.

WILL Braun finished his conversation with Officer Lacey Moller and hit the end button. They had agreed on a central point—a research lab—to meet so her team could escort him back to their ship. He moved to stand, but all the lights blinked off. Braun froze in place.

Hmm...

Seconds ticked by while Braun stood in the darkness. All he heard were the click and whine of his eyes failing to find enough light to focus.

It was concerning.

A rising sense of dread came up from the pit of his stomach, but he told it to settle, that it wasn't yet time to panic.

Fear was an invader, threatening to come in and set him screaming, but Braun knew—*he knew*—that this was once more fate playing a cruel joke. Again testing him to see if he was an uneven man who doubted himself, or if he truly believed in his purpose.

He straightened his back, took a deep, stale breath, and exhaled. Here, in the darkness, alone with only his thoughts and the clicks of his mechanical eyes, he was still a man of principle.

Still certain of who he was.

The lights came back on, just as he knew they would, and he looked back to the control panel. He clicked through a few screens and understood that this was just a reboot. The system was trying to work out where the breaches were, quadrant by quadrant.

That or the entire thing is taking its last gasps.

That wasn't the case, of course. Or it might be, but it would surely hold out until Braun was off the station. Regardless, he didn't like the idea of being caught in the dark with one of those things, so he clicked through the cameras confirming there was nothing in his way.

Don't take too long, or Rodney and the others' sacrifice will have been in vain.

Assured of his safety, he headed out. He pressed commands on the door, and it slid open. The irritating water quickly rushed in.

Oh. I'd almost forgotten.

It was quite miserable walking around in wet shoes and cold feet while breathing this terrible air.

He heard a faint scream from the direction of the sector chief's cabin and decided his predicament could be worse.

Braun trudged forward to the research lab. Though he'd never personally been there, he had read the reports. They were mildly intriguing. Their goal was terraforming Mars, something colonists had been aspiring to accomplish for decades. It was a secure room, and Braun had seen through the cameras that it was still unoccupied.

Something groaned ahead of him, and Braun dove into a nearby bathroom. He stayed there, hiding in silence and listening carefully as it passed.

By the sounds of it, he believed it to be one of the *ridden*, the creatures Lesliann had so aptly named.

Braun noted how fortunate it was such creatures made no attempt to be quiet.

Several minutes after the creature had passed, he went to a urinal and relieved himself. Dutifully, he pressed down the lever to flush and headed back into the hallway.

Twice more he ducked into adjoining rooms, mildly irritated at the passing creatures, before he found the lab.

It was one of several that was actually built on top of the Felicity base. He had to take a short set of stairs to get there.

When he got to the door, he let it scan his face, and was pleasantly surprised when it opened. There were no windows here, and thankfully, no water. But it was cold and drearily dark.

"Full lights," Braun said, and the room suddenly became much brighter.

And while he had read the reports on the research done here, he'd never seen it firsthand. The terraforming of Mars required native animals, and while most of the research and engineering was done on Earth, some modifications were done here.

Large incubators filled with liquid housed an assortment of animals and creatures Braun had never seen before, but he could clearly see their inspiration. One looked like a strange variation of a cow.

The thought of *Mars cows* made Braun smirk.

But they were dead. All dead. Their machinery was non-critical, and when the power went down, so did their life support.

Braun turned from it and sat down at the computer terminal, logging in with his credentials. He once more took controls of the cameras, intent to see how well his rescuers were doing.

As soon as he opened up the program, the last viewed camera came on.

A man was screaming in a room. It was hard for Braun to tell who it was—likely one of the scientists who had woken up with him from cryo but had stayed behind when they split the group. The memory of some of their faces were a bit vague to him.

The man had fallen to his ass, backpedaling from something Braun couldn't see. Braun swiveled the camera for a better view. The man must have noticed as he started waving at the camera, screaming desperately at it, though he was silent to Braun.

What exactly is it he thinks I can do for him?

Braun was in the middle of taking a breath before he stopped short.

A creature with stout, powerful legs and a thick, fat tail waddled into view. It had small arms that dangled in front of it and a mouth as large as its gut.

But atop its scalp was a dangling, human face.

What in God's name is that?

Braun passively rubbed his chin as he watched the scene unfold.

The man in the room desperately jumped and waved at the camera, wasting his last moments of life with foolish antics.

Scalpie.

That name strangely came to Braun's mind. He watched as it cornered the man, and Braun noted that it seemed to enjoy the panic it induced.

Giving up on whomever may or may not be watching on the other end of the camera, the man made one hopeless attempt to run past Scalpie, but it jumped on him, surprisingly agile for a creature of its size. The man slammed into the ground, and Scalpie placed its foot on his chest as it leaned over him.

Braun expected a quick bite, something that would end this man's poor suffering.

Instead, Scalpie dragged its coarse tongue across his face. It ripped off chunks of flesh, and the man moved and shook, uselessly fighting to get free.

Braun imagined the screams must have been loud.

Horrible as it was, Braun continued to watch as Scalpie licked the man's face off and exposed all the blood and bone beneath. When it was entirely gone, and only then, Scalpie casually bit half of the man's head off.

There must be a reason. Why would it do such a thing? Intentional cruelty? Doubtful.

Intrigued, Braun couldn't turn away. He only watched as Scalpie knelt down, and the human face on its head began to crack and move.

Is it adjusting to look like the man's?

Again, Braun was unsure, but he was certain of one thing.

They are evolving.

There had been no relief.

"Get it! Get it! Aim for its goddamn face!"

They'd only just gotten out of the cafeteria before the creatures—large, inhuman aliens—had descended on them.

"The vent! They're coming out of the vent!"

Tealson heard the cries, but had no idea who was doing the shouting. It wasn't clear over the sounds of gunfire.

These were not the infected citizens of Felicity, but creatures from another reality.

One had bounded forward, as thick as a horse and with powerful legs. Its mouth flayed open as if it had three jaws in a tight triangular shape. It roared, spit flying from its mouth.

Tealson fired several rounds directly into its gut.

Everyone took action. Everyone fought.

Each step Tealson took on his skinned foot burned and ached more than the last. The boot they had taken off one of the creatures had been cold and wet. It made him feel as if thousands of little needles jabbed into his skin. But he barely noticed it with adrenaline dumping into his veins.

"Hold the line!" Tealson yelled as they pumped rounds into the horse-like creature.

When it fell dead, Tealson waved his arm forward, and they rushed to take cover behind it.

We're winning.

Impossibly, they were.

The creatures were being pushed back.

A smaller alien with long, pointed legs and arms burst from a vent. Its tail whipped around behind it, and it let out a shriek. They'd all turned on it and pumped enough rounds to send it quivering to the ground.

DalBon dared forward and stomped his boot down onto the alien's head, cracking it and making the whole body shrivel up. "Eat shit!" he yelled before he stomped again with a sickening crunch.

Tealson waved his crew forward, and the creatures retreated. "Give 'em hell!"

Moller screamed, "I'm out!" And Tommy handed her another pistol mag.

The creatures retreated, and everyone began to hoot and holler.

"Pussies!" Becks yelled at their backs.

"Where the hell do you think they're going?" Tommy asked as he reloaded. "They couldn't have given up that easy, right?"

"Don't know, and don't care to find out," Tealson said. He'd had enough of this whole damn place. "Let's just go get our boy."

BRAUN SAT AT THE TERMINAL, tapping his fingers impatiently. Watching the vid-screens, he knew he'd made the right decision to wait for an escort as he saw the crew fight their way toward him.

It would have been considerably difficult to get to them.

But that wasn't what was concerning him at the moment. He'd taken his eyes off the crew for a short time and flipped to the gate room.

It was repowering.

If Braun had been a weaker man, one threatened by setbacks and obstructions, his jaw might have dropped there. He might have curled into a ball or held his head into his hands.

But he was not a weaker man.

Interesting.

The gate was powering up once more. He had damaged it with Dixie, but it hadn't lasted. He had been concerned that overloading the conduit might not last, and now his concerns were realized.

It was possible the power rebooting had evened it out.

He considered what this meant as he waited for his rescuers.

After a time, the door opened, and the crew filed in. Braun stood to greet them.

They'd clearly been through a warzone, as the barrels of some of their rifles were still smoking. Their armor was smeared in black blood. They were breathing hard, and one of them turned to close the door as quickly as possible.

Seven in total, Braun noted. Each in CAG except for Miss Moller.

"Hello," Braun said to them, putting on his most polite smile. "We will need to—"

"Are you Braun?" one of the smaller men stepped forward and pointed a finger at him.

"Yes, I am."

"Great. Get your ass over here, we're leaving." The man waved him over.

"Shut up, Elliot." Another stepped forward. "I'm Commander Tealson. We're here to extract you. Gather whatever you need, and let's get the hell out of here."

Braun held a finger to his lips, considering. "There's been a problem."

"Don't know, don't care. Let's get the hell out of here," Elliot said, and this time Tealson didn't interrupt.

"No, it's not that simple." Braun motioned to the monitor. "Commander, care to take a look?"

Tealson huffed and headed over to the screen. "What the hell am I looking at here?"

Braun pointed at the gate. "Do you see this? This is where the creatures are coming from. While it's active, more are coming in. I'm afraid we must disable it before we can leave."

Tealson went quiet, staring at the screen.

Another man spoke, "Who gives a shit? We aren't actually considering doing anything besides leaving, are we?"

"I'm thinking, Becks," Tealson said, still looking at the screen. 'Where the hell are they coming from?"

"We—" Braun made a jabbing motion with his finger. "—punched a hole into another reality. They are coming through that hole. Cronux. That's what we call them. You could consider them an alien species." Braun tried to speak simply. He didn't expect these men to understand the complexities.

Tealson shook his head. "Look, whatever the hell it is—"

Feeling the direction of the conversation, Braun interrupted, "You don't understand. If we leave and that gate is still open, things will keep coming through. *I don't know what will happen.*"

Tealson went quiet again, looking at the screen. "Reeves, come here and take a look at this."

Tommy stepped toward the screen.

All at once, the power dropped. The computer screens, the lights, and even the emergency lights all died.

Braun was bathed in darkness.

The crew started panicking and asking questions, too many at once to understand. Each turned on their head lamps and looked around frantically.

One.

"What the fuck? Did *they* do this?"

Two.

"Shit! I can't see anything. My lamp isn't working. It got damaged in the—"

Three.

"Not this shit again. *Not this again.*"

Braun had counted. Steadying his breathing. When the power had gone out, he had felt his mind start to turn with fear, but he caught it and held it under control.

The others were afraid, but he was not.

He was not a man easily made afraid.

"*Quiet,*" Braun hissed. "It's a full system reboot."

"Reeves, what the hell is that?" Elliot asked.

"System in this sector is resetting. It could last a few minutes, but up to a half-hour."

"You sure that's all it is?" someone else asked.

Braun interrupted with a laugh. "I certainly hope so. If it's not, the whole station is going to decompress, and we're going to bleed air quickly."

Still grinning, Braun added, "But that'll be more of a problem for me than for the rest of you."

13

THEY'D TAKEN off Smith's arm, just below the shoulder. Alice had left him as much as she possibly could. But even that was a polite way of saying it.

Sawed-off.

Smith had passed out, making it all the easier. She wasn't sure she would've been able to do it if his eyes were open and looking at her.

The spinning blade had come to life, purring like a kitten. The high-intensity blade spun at incredible speeds. Bartlet had remarked it looked eerily like a simple attachment for his cordless screwdriver back at home. When she had pressed it to Smith's open flesh, it had made an awful grinding noise, like when her father had cut wood with his circular saw.

It had cut through the muscle with ease, spitting up bits of tissue and specks of blood. It wasn't until it got to bone that Alice had trouble. She had to push her weight against it until the bone bowed and cracked. Finally, she'd burst through it. As soon as the arm had come loose, she'd moved it away and had cracked open a flexible bandage wrap designed for battlefield wounds. It had looked like a piece of wax paper, but as soon as she'd worked it right over the stump, it had crinkled in, sealing itself and catching blood.

"This fucking thing!" Bartlet had shouted.

Alice had looked to see the severed arm, blood leaking from it, but the fingers were twitching and wisps were peeking out of the meat of the bicep, reaching for more arm to crawl into. The open air was confusing, and after a few moments, the fat parasite bubbled up to the edge.

Bartlet had lost control and smashed it with the butt of his rifle. It popped like a ripe mosquito.

Alice couldn't remember a more horrifying experience. But through it all her hands had been steady, her breathing relaxed, her voice level, and her pulse consistent.

Calm. She'd been calm.

It was only now, as Alice slid on her CAG gloves and picked up her rifle, that her heart beat like a drum. She watched Bartlet heft Smith's unconscious body onto his shoulder, and she choked down the panic.

"Let's go."

She ran ahead to the docking bay door. With the system reboot, the security system was functioning now. Instantly, a scanner sent green light over her face.

The light on the door blinked red.

"Override," Alice commanded. "Orbital command, emergency medical."

The door scanned the badge on her chest.

"*Access granted*," it said as the doors slid open.

Alice turned back to Bartlet, getting on the other side of Smith and wrapping her arm around his waist to help lift him as they rushed forward. She'd put her CAG gloves in one of her suit's pouches, and now regretted not having the added strength in her grip.

It'll be fine, just hold tight.

When they got to the ship, Alice commanded it to open. It groaned awake and lowered the access hatch.

After they went through decontamination and carried Smith in, Bennie rushed toward them, his boots stomping on the metal grating of the ship. "Whoa, whoa! What happened?"

"Hold on a minute, Bennie," Alice said, and they dragged him toward medical.

Bennie frowned. "He's not going to lose his shit like Burns, is he?"

"*No,*" she shouted back.

Bartlet and Alice carried Smith the rest of the way in, his boots dragging against the floor. They stepped past the broken examination table Mike had torn apart and heaved Smith onto the only remaining one. Alice sat her rifle into a corner as she went to work.

"Let's get the CAG off and strap him in tight. I don't think he needs it, but we better do it anyway." Alice said as she started working the clasps. "Just to be on the safe side of things."

"Good," Bartlet said absentmindedly.

They popped off the CAG and tossed the pieces of armor aside. She ran straps across Smith's torso, buckling them into place and adjusting them tightly. Alice noticed Bartlet's eyes—suddenly distant, an endless look in his stare. He was gazing at the stump of Smith's arm and began whispering to himself, slowly shaking his head from side to side. He jerked away and walked around the far side of the table to tighten the furthest straps.

He can't take much more.

Alice took a step back from the table and popped the clasps on her helmet. Air burst as she lifted it off and set it aside. "Bartlet, I need you to focus, okay?"

He turned slowly as if he had barely heard anything she'd said. "This is bull shit. Un-fucking-real."

"Bartlet, are you—"

"I'm all right," he cut her off. "I'll be okay."

Alice rolled over a cart with various medical tools and scanners attached, placing sensors on Smith's chest to monitor his vitals. She got out a syringe and loaded it with sedatives, injecting it into Smith's veins. They needed to draw his body out of shock before they put him into cryo.

"Listen," she said, turning her attention to Bartlet. "I know we've seen some bad things. We've been through hell, but we're almost out of here. I can give you a sedative to help with—"

"Winters, we need you to report to the bridge. Now." It was the voice of the pilot, Linda Stalls, over the local ship comms.

Bartlet looked from Smith to Alice. "Is he going to be okay here?"

"Yeah," Alice said. "He's going to be out for a while. After that," she sighed. "He's not going to be a happy camper, that's for sure." Alice looked down at Smith, praying she'd done enough for him.

You've done all you can.

"Let's go to the bridge," she said.

"No. I'm going to my room," Bartlet said and marched out, popping the clasps of his helmet as he left the room.

She watched him leave, holding a breath. When he was gone, she glanced once more to Smith and then left the room.

She took the lift to the command level, hearing her steps on the grating as she headed toward the bridge. Now that she was inside the ship, her whole body felt heavy and tired, but it was nice to breathe clean air without the helmet. Stalls and Bennie were there. They instantly turned to her as she came up.

"What do you need?" Alice asked. "Where's Moller?"

"Not important right now," Stalls said.

Bennie pointed in the direction she came. "You brought *another one* on board?"

Alice gawked. "I amputated his fucking arm, Bennie. What do you want me to do? Leave him on Felicity to be eaten by those things?"

"For shit's sake, Alice." Stalls shrugged. "What are you thinking?"

Alice sneered. "I got the parasite. *I got it.* I had to take off his entire damn arm, but I got it. *He's fine.*"

"Look." Bennie held his hands up defensively. "Nothing against Smith. I like him as far as carnie rednecks go, but we're not putting everyone at risk. We need to—"

Stalls cut in, "We need to ice him, Alice. Stick him in cryo. Now. I'll feel a whole lot better about having him on board if he's a popsicle."

Alice crossed her arms tightly in front of her, shaking her head. "We can't. We have to let his body calm down. He has to—"

"You got him sedated, Alice!" Stalls was shouting now and pointing at the hallway. "He's fucking calm. *I'm* the one who's not calm."

"Who is the goddamn medical professional here?" Alice shouted at Stalls. "It's not just having him calm. His body is in shock. We have to let his whole body cool down and adjust before we put him into cryo. He just had an amputation! We stick him in cryo now, and it could stop his heart."

Stalls shoved a finger at Alice. "I'm the ranking officer while the Commander is gone. So you do what I—"

"*No*," Alice cut her off, shaking her head. "I still have priority control over patients." She aimed a thumb at her chest. "*I get to decide their treatments, not a ranking officer.*"

"Hey, hey, hey," Bennie said, stepping between them, holding his arms out as if he were a ref between two boxers. "Listen, we need to be calm about this and—"

"Oh, shove it up your ass, Bennie." Stalls waved him off. "Yeah, she's a doctor, but she doesn't have a degree in fucking. . ." Stalls shook her head, searching for a word. "Alien, parasite, biology." She stared daggers at Alice, but her voice was calm. "You put us all at risk bringing him on board like that, especially after what we saw happened to Burns."

"I'll watch him, all right?" Alice shot back. "I'd do the same for you."

"Do me a favor. Don't." Stalls huffed. "That happens to me, don't cut my arm off. Shoot me in the fucking head."

Bennie started, "What we need to do is—"

"I didn't sign up for this." It was Bartlet. He'd come so quietly that no one had seen him enter or heard the door open. They all jumped and looked at him. The tone of his voice and the look on his face had all changed. "This isn't what we're supposed to be doing." Tyler grinned, but it was painful to look at. "No one signed up for any of this." He'd peeled off the upper portions of his CAG, but he was still wearing a drenched undershirt.

And he still had his rifle.

"Yo, hey, man." Bennie glanced over at Alice and Stalls both. "How about you put that down?"

Alice could see that the distant look in his eyes had shifted. His pupils were dilated.

I think he took something...

"You didn't see them, Bennie. They crawl right up inside you. We had to cut Smith's arm off." Bartlet wasn't making eye contact. His eyebrows were up, confused, as he looked across the floor. "Do you know what that was like? It's this fat, little, purple thing. It shivers and moves, and it wants to get *inside* you. We cut his whole arm off, and it —*the entire arm*—kept moving. The fingers were twitching until I smashed it. They get inside you, and they take over." He laughed. "They use you like a fucking puppet."

"Bartlet," Stalls said in a calm voice, though Alice could see she was tense. "You're starting to scare us."

"Scare you?" Bartlet looked over at them. "*Why?* What the hell do you have to be scared of? You two stayed on the ship. You sat right here. You could leave at any minute. I'm the security officer, so that means I just make sure none of you assholes steal anything. I usually just mop the damn floor. I'm fucking useless to you people." He pointedly gestured toward them with his rifle. "I didn't want to go out there but you kept making me go. *You kept* making *me go.*"

Bennie chuckled uncomfortably and rubbed his chest. "I didn't make you do *shit*, buddy." Bennie looked over at Stalls. "We were just talking, too—saying we don't want to be here either. We all just want to get the hell out of here, right?" Stalls gaze started to flicker away toward the computer screens.

"Everyone wants to get off this rock," Alice said. "We're not going to go out there anymore. You can rest now. How about you just hand us the rifle, and I give you something to calm down?"

A string of snot dripped out of Tyler's nose and down his lip. He wiped it off with the back of his hand and blinked hard. His eyes were red and distant. "I am calm, Winters. But I'm holding onto my goddamn gun until we're off Mars. Maybe forever." He laughed, a cold soulless sound.

With a smile that didn't touch his eyes, Bennie pointed at a nearby bench. "Just take it easy over there, buddy. No need to be walking around—"

"What the hell is that?" Stalls said, startling them all. She glanced away from a computer screen. "Something just opened the access hatch."

EPILOGUE

Scalpie was different from most of his kind. He did enjoy the screams the men made as he ate them, but that was not unique. Bursts of joy from their shared hive mind were common when the men were screaming or running or dying.

No, he was unique for entirely other purposes.

He was an engine of evolution.

Born in the old world, he had been the first of his brood to crack through his shell and crawl up to the surface, collapsing in an exhausted heap. It was not easy to exist on this world, and the weak would soon die.

Scalpie was not weak.

His brothers had come behind him, cracking through their shells and slumping down in exhaustion.

Some were so weak they had simply lain there as he fell upon them, tearing out the tender flesh of their throats and chewing their still-functioning organs.

There was no hate, no emotion to it. Only desire and necessity.

Feed.

His brothers' meat fed him and made him strong. Some resisted, fighting him for the chance of life, but they too fell, and they too were consumed.

Scalpie had scars from his brood that would be with him forevermore. Testaments to the harsh existence of this world.

It had taken days to end them all. Long battles had tested his strength and viciousness.

But when they were all dead and only he remained, his mother spoke to him.

Not with words—for they had none—but with feelings.

Go. Serve.

Those were the only things she'd ever said to him, but he recognized the honor bestowed upon him to have her say such, to have had her presence within him, to join the hive mind. To *know* her in such a way.

It was a blessing, and he roared in triumph and glee to have felt it.

He hadn't seen his mother, only felt her, and he was likely to never see or feel her again, but that was not important.

Obedience was all that mattered.

Driven by instinct, he'd raced with powerful legs toward a bleeding hole in reality, and he threw himself through it.

War had come immediately, and in the cold new world, he found prey far less resistant to him than his brothers.

He had fed upon them.

Men.

Scalpie had known this instinctually, knowing what the hive mind knew.

They had scattered and ran, and when they dwindled, Scalpie found it harder to find them.

"Access!" Scalpie had heard one of them saying, and a green light had shone across the man's face. A door had opened, and the man had gotten inside. He'd been behind a wall that Scalpie could not get through, no matter how strongly he attacked it.

The men were safe, but not for long. For he was an engine of evolution, wasn't he? Adapting to the needs of the hunt.

Scalpie found another man and held him down. The man screamed as Scalpie dragged his tongue across the man's face, the thick bristles of his tongue shredding the meat off as he carefully carved out what he needed.

This hadn't been for cruelty, but for necessity.

When all was done, the bones and structure on Scalpie's head began to shift and change, cracking painfully as new cartilage grew and rearranged.

He'd grown a flap of skin that inflated with blood when desired.

But that had been it. There had been no other men. For long months, there was nothing. Only the cold metal. The gate had even gone down. How or why, he didn't know and was not concerned.

Scalpie had taken to eating more of his brothers. They fought for their right to life, but he was strong, and they were weak.

He'd cracked them open and had eaten their pulsing organs.

Time went on, and the lights and power had come back on. Things had changed.

He'd been brought to a man that was already dead, a man in black armor that was strong and hard to chew. His lesser brothers had already removed the man's helmet when Scalpie happened upon them, and they allowed Scalpie to approach.

He collected the face.

Scalpie left again, seeking men behind closed doors. He found another set of doors, one where he could feel people behind them.

He moved to one of those doors, and a green light shined across him. A light blinked red.

It was locked, and would remain so.

But Scalpie was different from the others.

Scalpie allowed blood to flow into the human face upon his head—inflating and giving shape to the cruel replica. He angled its eyes to the light and patiently waited. It was a floppy, saggy mess of skin, but the cartilage and bones tightened and filled with blood, taking the shape of the face of the scientist he had eaten.

"Akshesh," Scalpie said with his thick tongue.

The light on the door blinked green. *"Access granted."*

Why did this work? Why was the light and the face necessary to opening doors? These were questions, but ones that Scalpie did not ask, for he did not concern himself with mysteries.

The door opened up, and Scalpie walked past words painted on the wall.

DOCKING BAY.

There was a large ship there, and Scalpie could sense people inside.

He did not know what this ship was or why it was here. He did not know of the people there, nor did he care about their intentions.

He had but one purpose.

Feed.

MORE CONTENT

Continue reading for the following extra content:

- Mars Twilight: *The Final Report of Marcie Robinson*
- Staff information: *Logs of the Perihelion*
- Cold War - Japan

And join Reality Bleed's exclusive discussion group to talk about the book with other readers!

Hope to see you there.

- Winter Gate Publishing

MARS TWILIGHT: THE FINAL REPORT OF MARCIE ROBINSON

Want to read notes and view drawings from a scientist that is losing her mind to a parasite? Head over to: https://tinyurl.com/MarsTwilight

LOGS OF THE PERIHELION

Go to **https://tinyurl.com/CrewLogs** to get this free bonus book and learn more of the Crew of the Perihelion.

BONUS CONTENT

The following is bonus content added for readers interested in knowing more about the world of Reality Bleed. It is not *required reading* but is only here as an add on.

We hope you enjoy it.

COLD WAR - JAPAN

A VIDEO ICON spun as it buffered, showing the image of a man smiling wide with a joint hanging from his mouth. The icon stopped spinning and the word *Start* displayed.

"And we're *live*," said the host, Joe Axel, a bald man with impressive muscles. He ran a popular interview show that had podcasts and videos.

Axel often interviewed people on mixed martial arts, stand up comedy, and just about any other subject. It wasn't uncommon for him to be high while he was doing it, either.

Today was different. Today he was clearly focused and interested.

But he was still going to get high.

"Hey there, folks," Axel said, staring into the camera as he leaned forward and spoke into his microphone. "We've got a great show lined up today. I'm going to be interviewing Dr. Jordan Robertson, Clinical Psychologist and Historian." He turned and gestured toward Jordan on the other side of the table. "Mr. Robertson, thank you for coming here."

Jordan, likewise wearing sound gear on his ears, tipped his head. "Thank you, Axel, it's a pleasure to be here."

"So Jordan," Axel went on. "You've been doing a series of videos and lectures on the Cold War lately and they've become pretty popular, but the one I wanted to talk to you about was your episode on *Japan*. All I can say about that is *wow*." Axel started fiddling with something beneath his desk. "Why'd you decide to focus so much on them?" He pulled out a joint from a drawer beneath his desk, and made a gesture to offer it to Jordan, who politely shook his hand.

Jordan smiled. "Yes, actually I saw a significant bump in traffic when you mentioned it on your show last week, I appreciate that. I decided to do a video specifically on them because of their importance in the Cold War, but also because the Japanese are a fairly extraordinary people. They went through their industrial revolution about a hundred years after the West, so you can imagine people very similar to samurai existing there not that long ago in the grand scheme of things. But after they did, they became quite the force to be reckoned with."

Axel's eyes widened with interest as he lit the joint and took a puff. "Hell yeah they did. Swords to machine guns and back again in almost no time."

Jordan nodded his head. "*And back again*, yes. They have extensive firearm laws in South Japan, and though there still are *some* firearms, it's also led to the use of knives and swords on occasion. Especially in gang warfare."

"Yakuza, brutal bastards with swords and shit. I love it." Axel grinned as he took another puff. "How about their mechanical parts? A lot of people have heard about it, but I actually saw it when I travelled there. It's not really something you can imagine until you've seen it. Pretty little college girl with all her fingers cut off." Axel was visibly shook.

"Right, mechanized limbs." Jordan waved out his hands. "Here in the West, we see these *mechanized limbs* mostly on wounded soldiers, or people who've had significant medical troubles, but in Japan it's far more common to see them in a fashionable sense."

Axel's eyebrows went up wide as he took a long drag of his joint. He exhaled smoke through his nose before speaking. "*Fashionable?*

That just seems insane to me. Why the hell would anyone want to do that?"

Jordan smiled and shrugged. "You see, with these mechanized limbs, you lose a lot of feeling. We've done a lot to connect the transmitters in fingertips directly to the spinal cord, but I'm told it's a constant *cold* feeling. You don't get the sensations you would with skin. Not to mention limb rejection is a very real thing. It's not uncommon to see people who've undergone the surgery of having a limb removed only to have their body reject the limb. I can imagine that would be particularly upsetting, though people still keep doing it.

"That isn't even it," Axel said, shaking his head now. "I did an interview with Dominic Lagonigro, this former Army Ranger guy—"

"He's the one that was injured in the Kudat raid, right?" Jordan asked. "I saw the medal ceremony."

Axel snapped his fingers. "Yep. Jumped on a heat frag to protect his unit. Melted his gear to his chest." Axel made a pained expression. "Anyway, he had to have his arms removed along with some chest muscles. He got it all replaced with—" Axel snapped his fingers again, this time trying to remember the word.

"Mechanized limbs," Jordan said, nodding.

"Yeah. He said it took six months of therapy and training just to learn how to do basic shit like feeding himself, and he's still working on driving. How the hell can the Japanese get around cutting pieces of themselves off, lose all that feeling and spend all that time trying to figure out how to use it again?"

"What can I say, they're a remarkable culture."

"Yeah, but as a clinical psychologist, *why?*" Axel prompted.

Jordan rubbed his gray beard. "A lot of reasons really. Historical reasons. You have to imagine the pure and utter *shock* the Japanese received when they were not only defeated, but divided in *half*. I mean, think about this, Joe, they believed their Emperor was a *god*, and when the country was split in two, he was kept in North Japan under the Russians. *Under house arrest.* They are a proud people, and just as the invasion was mounting the words *a million lives for the Emperor* was on everyone's lips. They trained their children to fight and they *did*. What utter insanity is that? Forget about kamikaze, and suicide bombers. Forget about the mothers handing their young sons knives to kill themselves with if they're captured. They trained their young children to fight the enemy. To *die* for the Emperor. And those children *did*. They *did* charge the enemy." Jordan threw his hands up. "And after all that, they still lost the Emperor!"

Axel had gone silent, his eyes wide as he leaned in. *"A million lives for the Emperor*, wow. How many do you think actually died?"

"During the invasion?" Jordan asked and Axel nodded. "Oh, rough estimates are—" Jordan popped some air through his mouth and slashed his hand. "Halved."

"Halved? You saying half the population of Japan died during the invasion?"

"Roughly. That is the estimate. Men. Women. Children. All fighting. All dying. *A million lives for the Emperor* was not a joke, though it was an underestimation. Perhaps thirty million lives would have been a better slogan."

"*Fuuuuck*," Axel said as he stuck the joint back into his mouth. "And you think that made them *cut pieces off themselves?*"

Jordan nodded. "Precisely. Something like that. As something like this happens to a society, it reverberates down to the individual. They see their Emperor, and he's a new Emperor at this point, but Emperor nonetheless, being puppeted in North Japan and they feel like they are *missing a piece of themselves.*" Jordan took a deep breath and held out his hand. "Of course, it's only a theory. It does seem to be a trend amongst a certain brand of Japanese. You don't find the average housewife doing it. I suppose it's more of a dissident thing."

"So the Emperor is in the North, who is running the South? They are a democracy, right?"

"Ehh." Jordan winced and shook a flat hand in front of him. "They have some elections, the American forces insisted on that. There is even a prime minister, but the man with the ruling power is the Shogun."

"Shogun?" Axel asked.

Jordan nodded his head. "More of a return to normalcy in Japan really. From the twelfth century to eighteen sixty eight, the shogun was the overlord of Japan, with the Emperor as the nominal leader."

"Why'd they stop in eighteen sixty eight?"

"Well." Jordan frowned. "I wouldn't say I know too much about this time period, but the idea was that the people believed that they had gotten weak and they wanted the Emperor to take control again like the *good-ole-days*, ignoring the fact that the *good-ole-days* were six hundred some years ago. The shogun was a hereditary position and they ruled for some time."

"All right, so they took him out, why'd they put him back in?"

"The *South Japanese* reinstated the Shogun. Supposedly of the same bloodline as the original. You see, the shogun, way back somewhere around a thousand years ago, weren't the leaders but just the chief military commanders. Now that the Emperor has been 'lost'—" Jordan made air quotes. "—they reinstated the military position to retrieve him. That has been the stated mandate of the Shogun for sometime now. Retrieve the Emperor. It's well known that both North and South Japan fund insurgent activities against each other."

"It's still crazy as all hell for me. Half their population gone? People cutting pieces off themselves? I can tell you, when I went to South Japan, it was fantastic. Everyone there is nice, everything is clean, girls are all pretty—"

"All on the surface, Axel." Jordan nodded. "I've been there too, they're very kind people. But you have to imagine there's a lot of hurt behind closed doors. That all said, South Japan has done very well for itself in its time post-war. They are a front-runner in technology. It's sad to see what North Japan has become."

"You heard the headline just today, right? Dozen or so refugees drowned when their boat collapsed." Axel sighed and shook his head. "It's horrifying to see such prosperity in some place like Osaka, and then to know just a few inches on the map, there are people dying by the thousands."

Jordan nodded empathetically. "Pretty much everywhere but Tokyo is starving in North Japan. They keep Tokyo pretty for the propaganda videos I suppose. The Russians wheel out the Emperor a few times a year, but he always looks terrible. The South Japanese media still covers any speeches or proclamations from the Emperor, but you can tell it's mostly just wounding for the Southern Japanese to see him so... Disheveled. A bleeding wound that refuses to heal."

"Do they see him as a god still?"

"No, not generally." Jordan shook his head. "There are likely still a few here and there that do, but I think he's just representative of something. But something we've always wondered is what would happen if he demanded the South to reform under the North? It's an honest question. I'm not sure what would happen."

Axel frowned hard. "What? You're not sure that they wouldn't just flip him off and tell him to eat shit?"

Jordan smirked and shook his head. "They very likely would, but he never has, despite several conflicts and engagements between the two countries."

"Why not? They are enemies after all. My grandfather even fought in the Japanese war."

"Couldn't tell you, Axel. I can only say what the suspicions are. And that is he refuses. We can easily suspect that the Russians lean on him, but it appears that he resists them. Though he often looks . . . distressed. *The Emperor holds and so do we*, another common expression. At least in the South."

"Wow, I could talk to you all day about the Japanese, and we haven't even gotten into all those crazy gang fights with swords you were telling me about earlier. So let's hold that thought while I go take a piss."

Jordan laughed.

An icon appeared on the screen of Axel smiling wide with a joint in his mouth.

CRASH. BURN. DIE.

REALITY BLEED BOOK 3

NIGHT TERRORS

REALITY BLEED BOOK 4

ABOUT J.Z. FOSTER

J.Z. Foster is a writer originally from Ohio. He spent several years in South Korea where he met and married his wife.

He received the writing bug from his mother, NYTimes best-selling author, Lori Foster.

Check out his other books and let him know how you like them!

Write him an email at:
JZFoster@JZFoster.com

ABOUT JUSTIN M. WOODWARD

Justin M. Woodward is an author from Headland, Alabama. He lives with his wife and two small boys. He has been writing since 2015.

He's had stories appear in various anthologies alongside authors like Stephen King and Neil Gaiman. His work has been featured in Scream Magazine.

You can keep up with him on social media, and on www.justinm-woodward.com

WINTER GATE PUBLISHING

Want to stay up to date on the latest from Winter Gate Publishing? Follow us on Facebook at Facebook.com/WinterGatePublishing to know more!

Copyright © 2020 by Winter Gate Publishing All rights reserved. No part of this book may be reproduced in any form or by any electronic or mechanical means, including information storage and retrieval systems, without written permission from the author, except for the use of brief quotations in a book review. This is a work of fiction. Names, characters, places, and incidents are a product of the author's imagination. Locales and public names are sometimes used for atmospheric purposes. Any resemblance to actual people, living or dead, or to businesses, companies, events, institutions, or locales is completely coincidental. Call of the Void / Winter Gate Publishing -- 1st ed.

Winter Gate Publishing. Reality Bleed: Call of the Void

Printed in Great Britain
by Amazon